Rocking Out

Joe was about to answer me when he was interrupted by an announcer's voice on the CD. *"Her name is Vee Sharp,"* said the voice. *"And she first hit the pop charts with her number one hit, 'Take It from Vee.'"*

On the screen, a Top Ten music chart appeared. A tiny star twinkled in the number one spot, then exploded into a huge starburst.

"Today," the voice continued, *"Vee Sharp is one of the hottest young stars on the music scene."*

Vee's beautiful face filled the screen.

"But it's hard to stay on top in the record business. Especially for someone like Vee Sharp. In spite of topping the charts with her hit songs and albums, Vee is in danger of having her career cut short."

Suddenly the music stopped. A giant red bull's-eye framed Vee's face.

"Because someone is trying to kill her."

THE HARDY BOYS

UNDERCOVER BROTHERS™

Available from Simon & Schuster

THE HARDY BOYS

UNDERCOVER BROTHERS™

 #8   Top Ten Ways to Die

FRANKLIN W. DIXON

Aladdin Paperbacks
New York   London   Toronto   Sydney

First Aladdin Paperbacks edition February 2006
Copyright © 2006 by Simon & Schuster, Inc.

ALADDIN PAPERBACKS
An imprint of Simon & Schuster
Children's Publishing Division
1230 Avenue of the Americas
New York, NY 10020

Designed by Lisa Vega
The text of this book was set in Aldine 401BT.
Printed in the United States of America
10 9 8 7 6 5 4

THE HARDY BOYS MYSTERY STORIES and HARDY BOYS
UNDERCOVER BROTHERS are trademarks of Simon & Schuster, Inc.
ALADDIN PAPERBACKS and colophon are trademarks of
Simon & Schuster, Inc.
Library of Congress Control Number: 2005903791

ISBN-13: 978-1-4169-0846-3
ISBN-10: 1-4169-0846-3

TABLE OF CONTENTS

1.

Weenies on Wheels

"Would you like relish with that?"

I pulled the steel tongs out of my apron pocket and plucked a plump pink wiener out of the steaming vat of water.

"Just a smear of mustard with a few dabs of ketchup," said the businessman, glancing at his watch. "And make it fast, kid."

I rolled my eyes.

It was bad enough that I was standing in the middle of Times Square wearing a stupid wiener-shaped hat and Rollerblades. It was even worse dealing with cranky New Yorkers and picky tourists.

"Here you go, sir. That'll be a dollar twenty-five."

The businessman blinked his eyes. "A dollar twenty-five? When did the price go up?"

My brother Frank pointed at the sign on the side of the street vendor cart. "The price is listed right here, sir," he said with a polite smile. "And it's worth every penny. You can't buy a better hot dog than Weenies on Wheels. We use only the finest meat products. Absolutely no fillers."

I looked at my brother—in his dorky hot-dog hat—and started laughing. I just couldn't help myself.

The businessman was not amused.

"It's a rip-off, kid."

He thrust the hot dog at me and stormed off.

I looked at Frank and held up the wiener. A thick glob of mustard dripped onto the sidewalk.

"Hungry?"

My brother scoffed. "After today, I don't think I'll ever eat a hot dog again."

"I'm with you, bro."

I gave him a little shove that sent him rolling backward.

Then someone screamed.

Loud.

"Help! HELP!"

Frank and I spun around on our Rollerblades.

Across the crowded sidewalk, a young woman with long dark hair stood screaming in front of an automated teller machine. She clutched a wad of twenty-dollar bills in her hand and shook her head back and forth.

"No! You can't have it! Get away!"

She struggled against her attackers—three teenage boys wearing black knit caps and Rollerblades.

"It's them, Joe," Frank whispered. "The ATM Rollers."

I recognized them instantly from the hidden-camera footage the ATAC team had sent us. The ATM Rollers had been terrorizing New Yorkers for weeks, targeting victims at cash machines in the Times Square area. Our mission was simple: go undercover, blend into the crowd, and keep an eye on the bank machines.

Frank and I were totally psyched about the assignment. It was our chance to hunt down criminals in the streets of New York.

How cool is that?

Then we got a look at the Weenies on Wheels wagon and the ridiculous hot-dog hats we had to wear.

Not so cool.

Hey, at least we were wearing Rollerblades.

And we were ready to roll.

"Freeze!" I yelled across the sidewalk at the thieves. "You're under arrest!"

The boys looked up and saw Frank and me blading toward them.

"Run for it!" shouted the tallest boy.

The three robbers released the girl—and took off down the sidewalk.

The chase was on.

Frank and I dug our Rollerblades into the concrete and zoomed off after them. Weaving back and forth, we made our way through a pack of stunned pedestrians. A woman with a baby carriage shrieked as I rolled toward her. With a fast twist, I swerved around them.

And smashed into a guy selling newspapers.

The man toppled backward, tossing an armload of *New York Post*s up into the air. One of the pages slapped me in the face, blocking my vision. I shook it off as quickly as I could. Then I skidded to a stop and looked around.

Where did they go?

The ATM Rollers were nowhere in sight. I glanced down Broadway, but all I could see was a mob of tourists in a long ticket line.

"Joe! This way!" my brother shouted.

Frank waved at me from across the street. Without skipping a beat, I charged after him—right into the middle of traffic.

Honk!

A yellow cab screeched to a halt. The front fender grazed my knee, almost knocking me down. Then a bearded cab driver stuck his head out the window and started shaking his fist at me.

"You idiot! Watch where you're going!"

"Sorry!" I shouted back.

Cars started beeping their horns at me. Traffic was backed up for blocks. Ducking down, I raced across the street and hopped up onto the sidewalk.

"Come on, Joe!" Frank yelled. "They're getting away!"

He pointed down Broadway. I caught a glimpse of the robbers' black knit caps as they bobbed and weaved through the crowds.

We took off after them.

Side by side we raced past tourists and street vendors, fire hydrants and parking meters, movie theaters and electronics stores. Faster and faster, closer and closer, we zoomed after our targets.

One of the robbers glanced over his shoulder and spotted us. His eyes widened as he realized how close we were. Then he did something that almost stopped us in our tracks.

He spun around and braced himself against a

street vendor's table full of New York City souvenirs. With a loud grunt, he flipped the whole thing over.

"Here you go, wieners!" he shouted. "Stop and shop!"

Dozens of souvenirs crashed and clattered across the sidewalk: Manhattan skyline snow globes, Empire State Building thermometers, "I ™ NY" T-shirts, and green Statue of Liberty hats.

"Look out!" Frank yelled.

We roller-bladed straight toward the pile of junk—at top speed.

Oh, no.

"Jump!" I hollered.

Frank and I jumped—up, up, and over—soaring through the air while onlookers screamed and cheered. The sidewalk was a blur beneath me, and I braced myself for a hard landing.

Crunch! Thump!

We made it.

But when I looked up, I saw the robbers skate around the corner onto Forty-second Street and disappear. Frank and I raced after them.

"Where did they go?" my brother asked.

"Down there!"

I pointed at the subway entrance.

And took off down the stairs.

"Easy, Joe!" Frank yelled.

It was too late to stop now.

K-thunk, k-thunk, k-thunk!

Our Rollerblades rattled down the stairs, banging hard with each step. I had to grab the handrail a couple of times to keep from bouncing off balance.

"Auuuugh!"

A little old lady shrieked as we bobbled past her. She even swung her purse at Frank but missed him.

When we reached the bottom of the stairs, we had to stop to let our eyes adjust to the darkness of the terminal. It didn't take us long to spot the ATM Rollers.

They were jumping the turnstiles and heading for the nearest train platform.

"After them!" Frank shouted.

Easier said than done. It was rush hour, after all, and the place was crawling with commuters. People rushed back and forth, blocking our path.

To make matters worse, I was still holding the hot dog. But I wasn't going to rush something as delicious as a hot dog.

Finally we managed to slip inside one of the exit gates, fighting our way through the crowd like salmon swimming upstream. I had to hold the hot dog against my apron so I wouldn't smear people with mustard and ketchup.

Within seconds we reached the platform.

"There they are," said Frank.

The three roller-bladers stood about fifty feet away, surrounded by the rush hour mob.

"We got them cornered," I said.

But I spoke too soon.

A subway train roared down the track, its brakes screeching as it stopped along the platform. Then the train doors slid open, and people started climbing aboard.

"We're going to lose them," said Frank.

"No, we're not."

I pushed Frank into one of the subway cars. The doors shut behind us, and the train started to move.

"Excuse me, ma'am. Excuse me, sir."

Slowly we crept our way toward the front of the car, careful not to roll across anyone's toes. Suddenly, without warning, the train slammed on its brakes. We rolled and pitched forward, grabbing the handrails for support.

"Hold on!"

The train pulled in to another stop. The doors slid open, and Frank grabbed my arm.

"They're getting out! Come on!"

I rolled after my brother onto the platform. I could see the ATM Rollers heading for the nearest stairway. We tried to race after them, but they were just too fast.

I was almost ready to give up. The three robbers were too far ahead of us. We'd never catch up.

But I was forgetting something: It's really hard to climb stairs in Rollerblades.

Ha!

The three boys had to turn their bodies and navigate each step sideways. It was pretty slow going.

And it was our last chance to stop them.

I lifted up the dripping hot dog—and hurled it as hard as I could.

It landed with a loud splat on one of the stairs.

And it tripped one of the robbers.

The boy yelped as his foot flew out from under him. Then he collapsed and slid down the stairs.

"Way to go, Joe!"

Frank cheered. Then he reached into his apron and grabbed his metal hot-dog tongs. With a quick toss, he sent the utensil flying through the air. It crashed with a metal *clang* into the Rollerblades of the second boy, who stumbled and fell.

Two down, one to go.

Frank and I reached the bottom of the stairs—and the third thief had almost reached the top. Quickly, I ripped off my Weenies on Wheels apron.

Then, swinging it in the air like a lasso, I threw the garment at the guy's left Rollerblade.

The apron strings caught on one of his wheels.

Yes!

And the boy came tumbling down.

"Nice one, bro," said Frank.

The ATM Rollers lay on the concrete stairs, groaning and rubbing their bruises.

"Nobody move!"

Frank and I looked up. A pair of transit cops stood at the top of the stairs. One of them pointed at the fallen roller-bladers.

"Look! It's the ATM Rollers!" he said to his partner.

The two cops reached for their handcuffs and started helping the boys to their feet.

Frank nudged me with his arm. "Let's get out of here before they start asking questions."

"Good idea."

Then, spinning around, we zoomed off down the platform. It was time to call the ATAC team and give them our report.

Mission accomplished.

But there was still one thing we had to do first: dump our dopey hot-dog hats into the nearest trash can.

2.
Top Ten Ways to Die

Okay. So we survived a high-speed roller blade chase through Times Square. Cool.

Now it was time to start acting like normal teenagers—or Mom and Aunt Trudy might get suspicious.

"That was so awesome, Frank," my brother said as we pulled our motorcycles into the driveway. "I still can't believe we jumped over all those souvenirs on the sidewalk. It must have been an eight-foot jump! At least!"

I pulled off my helmet and smiled. "Definitely awesome, Joe," I agreed. "Now it's time to chill out—and get our stories straight. We were in New York City to see the Vee Sharp concert. Got it?"

"Got it."

11

We climbed off our bikes and walked through the front door—just in time to see the evening news on TV. Mom, Dad, and Aunt Trudy were **glued to the set.**

"The ATM Rollers are now safely behind bars," said a woman reporter. "But the police still don't know the identities of the heroic street vendors who chased them down. Thanks to these two mystery men on wheels, Times Square is a safer place to see a show, ride a subway, or grab a hot dog . . . with or without relish. This is Connie Kung reporting."

The reporter took a bite of a frankfurter and saluted the camera.

Dad looked up and winked at Joe and me.

As founder of American Teens Against Crime, he knew about our latest mission. And as a former cop, he knew how dangerous the mission could have been. That wink let us know that he was proud of us—without letting Mom and Aunt Trudy in on our little secret. "Frank! Joe! You're home!" said Mom with a smile.

Aunt Trudy glanced up from her knitting. "So how was the concert, boys?" she asked. "Did you enjoy Dee Sharp?"

"*Vee* Sharp," I corrected her. "And yes, she put on an amazing show."

Aunt Trudy straightened her glasses. "Really? I

was reading about her in one of those magazines at the beauty parlor. It said she lip-synchs."

I shrugged. "Maybe during some of the big dance numbers."

Aunt Trudy shook her head and clucked her tongue. "I just don't understand music today. It seems like nobody can really sing. It's all faked in the studio. These so-called 'singers' just move their mouths with the music during their concerts. It's shameful. Now, in *my* day . . ."

Ding.

Saved by the doorbell.

"I'll get it." Joe walked over to the door and opened it.

A deliveryman stood in the doorway holding a medium-size box. "Package for Frank and Joe Hardy. Sign here, please."

Joe signed the paper on the man's clipboard and accepted the package. Then he thanked the delivery-man and shut the door.

Aunt Trudy put down her knitting and walked over to investigate. "What's this?" she asked, squinting through her glasses.

You could say she's a bit of a snoop. I guess it must run in the family.

Joe held up the package. The sides were covered with silhouettes of CDs and musical notes. "It's from the Top Ten Music Club," he said, reading the return address on the label.

"Send it back."

It was Mom. She had come up behind us and now glared down at the package with a disapproving look.

"You boys joined one of those music CD clubs, didn't you?" she said.

I shot Joe a look. I could tell he was thinking the same thing I was thinking: The package probably contained our next mission from the ATAC team.

Joe and I were both too smart to join a music CD club. Our friend Chet had signed up for one of them last year, and he was still trying to pay off his debt.

But I had no choice but to play along.

"Sorry, Mom," I said. "But they give you ten CDs for only a dollar!"

Mom shook her head. "Yes, but then you have to buy five or six more CDs at their 'regular' price—which is twice the store price. It's highway robbery."

"And worse yet," said Aunt Trudy, "they target foolish innocent teenagers."

"Oh, let's not carried away," said Dad, stepping into the conversation. "Frank and Joe are neither foolish nor innocent. If they made a mistake by joining this music club, they'll simply have to pay the price."

He gave me another wink.

Mom shrugged. She could never argue against us learning a lesson firsthand.

"Thanks, Dad," I said.

Joe nudged my arm. "Come on, Frank. Let's check out our new CDs."

He grabbed the box and we ran upstairs two steps at a time.

"That was close," said Joe when we reached my bedroom. "I thought Mom was going to make us send back our next mission from ATAC."

We walked through the door—and were almost knocked over with a flapping of wings.

"ATAC! ATAC! ATAC!"

It was our parrot, Playback, flying over our heads to greet us.

"ATAC!"

"Knock it off, Playback," Joe said with a snort. "Mom and Aunt Trudy will think we're being *attacked*."

Finally Playback settled down. I went to my desk and fired up the computer while Joe grabbed a pair of scissors to open the box.

"Dude! Check it out!"

Joe opened the box and pulled out a pair of tiny MP3 players with cordless earphones and a silver pocket pen that looked like something out of a *Star Wars* movie.

"I wonder what this does?" said Joe.

"Don't touch it," I warned him. "You might blow the house up or something. Let's wait until we hear our instructions first, okay?"

"Okay, Mr. Safety."

Joe reached inside the box again. This time, he pulled out a bunch of magazines and posters and music CDs and other stuff.

"Frank! Look who it is!"

Joe unrolled one of the posters. Smiling back at me was a giant head shot of pop superstar Vee Sharp. Blonde, beautiful, and beyond famous, she was one of the hottest new artists in the record industry. You couldn't turn on the radio without hearing one of her songs.

"But wait, there's more," said Joe, imitating a corny TV infomercial.

He held up the magazines one by one: *Pop Teen*, *Music Now*, *Veejay Digest*, *Rock 'n' Reel*.

Vee Sharp was featured on every one of them.

"Maybe this *isn't* from ATAC," said Joe. "Maybe Aunt Trudy ordered all this stuff for us because she thought we were big fans."

I reached for CDs and started reading the covers on the plastic cases. "It looks like we have a complete collection of her albums here. *My*

Name Is Vee Sharp. Vee Day. Sharp Attack. Top Ten Ways to Die. Say La Vee . . ."

"Wait a minute," Joe interrupted.. "*Top Ten Ways to Die*? That's not one of her albums."

I looked at my brother and smirked. "Why, Joe. I didn't know you were such a big Vee Sharp fan."

Joe blushed. "Well, you have to admit she has some cool songs."

"You *are* a fan, aren't you?" I teased.

Hey, if you can't tease your little brother, who *can* you tease?

"No, I'm not a fan," Joe protested. "But she's not bad if you like dance music."

"I thought you liked punk and rock, Joe."

"I do, but . . ."

"Admit it, Joe. You *love* Vee Sharp, don't you?"

"No!"

"Yes, you do! Joe loves Vee Sha-arp! Joe loves Vee Sha-arp!"

I started singing it over and over, poking my brother with my fingers. "Joe loves Vee Sha-arp!"

"Knock it off!" he growled, wrestling me to the floor.

Soon Playback joined in, flapping his wings and squawking, "Joe loves Vee Sha-arp! Joe loves Vee Sha-arp!"

Suddenly there was a knock at the door.

"Are you boys all right in there?"

It was Dad. He opened the door and stuck his head inside.

My brother and I tried to look innocent—even though Joe had me in a headlock.

Dad ignored our wrestling position. "I just wanted to say good job, boys. I was a little worried about you taking on those ATM Rollers in New York."

I shrugged. "It was nothing, Dad."

If you think roller-blading down stairs and into the subway at rush hour is nothing.

Dad nodded and started to leave. But then he stopped. "Oh, one more thing," he added. "That girl you saved at the cash machine? She called you guys 'heroes' on the news. And she said one of you was 'especially cute.'"

He closed the door behind him.

"She was referring to me," said Joe.

"Was not."

"Was too."

"Well, if she meant you, she's wasting her time," I said. "Because Joe loves Vee Sha-arp! Joe loves Vee Sha-arp!"

After a few more minutes of wrestling, we managed to calm down and pop the *Top Ten Ways to Die* CD into my computer. Joe pulled a chair up to the desk. The monitor went black and music started pumping through the speakers.

It was Vee Sharp, of course.

The pop star's breathy voice sang out over the bouncing chords and heavy beat. I immediately recognized her first big hit, "Take It from Vee."

When the young singer reached the rap part of the song, Playback squawked and flapped his wings.

"See?" said Joe. "Even parrots like her music."

"What does that say about *you*?"

Joe was about to answer me when he was interrupted by an announcer's voice on the CD. *"Her name is Vee Sharp,"* said the voice. *"And she first hit the pop charts with her number one hit, 'Take It from Vee.'"*

On the screen, a Top Ten music chart appeared. A tiny star twinkled in the number one spot, then exploded into a huge starburst.

"Today," the voice continued, *"Vee Sharp is one of the hottest young stars on the music scene."*

Vee's beautiful face filled the screen.

"But it's hard to stay on top in the record business. Especially for someone like Vee Sharp. In spite of topping the charts with her hit songs and albums, Vee is in danger of having her career cut short."

Suddenly the music stopped. A giant red bull's-eye framed Vee's face.

"Because someone is trying to kill her."

3.

Snap, Crackle, Pop Star

Kill Vee Sharp?

I looked over at Frank, then glanced down at the music poster on the floor.

Why would anyone want to kill Vee Sharp?

The computer screen faded to black. A tiny white square appeared, growing larger and larger until it filled the screen. It was a letter of some sort. But the words had been clipped out of magazines and newspapers and glued to the page.

Like a hostage note.

"Last week Ms. Sharp received this message in her fan mail," the announcer told us.

Frank and I leaned forward in our chairs to read the scary-looking letter.

At the top, it said: TOP TEN WAYS TO DIE.

And underneath, it read: NUMBER 10: ELECTRO-CUTION.

"*The next day,*" the voice continued, "*this is what happened during Vee's concert in San Diego.*"

The image on the screen dissolved into live video footage of a large outdoor stadium. The camera zoomed over the heads of screaming fans and focused in on a microphone at center stage. A red curtain opened and out stepped Vee Sharp. The fans went wild.

First she danced around to the drumbeats. Then she approached the microphone stand and reached out her hand.

Zap!

The microphone snapped and crackled. Electrical sparks flew from the mike and showered onto the stage.

Vee jumped back. A bolt of electricity shot out of the cord.

Whump!

A large speaker exploded.

The road crew ran onto the stage with fire extinguishers. Somebody grabbed Vee by the shoulders and pulled her back behind the curtain.

Then the screen faded to black.

I glanced at Frank. "Man, this is serious," I said.

My brother nodded.

21

Another tiny square appeared on the screen.

"A few days later Ms. Sharp received a second message," said the announcer.

The square grew and grew until we could read the cut-and-pasted words on the note.

NUMBER 9: FIRE.

The image dissolved again. A shaky handheld camera revealed a dressing-room door with Vee Sharp's name on it. Thick black smoke billowed from the room.

"The next day, Ms. Sharp's wardrobe was set on fire," said the announcer. *"And this event was quickly followed by a third message."*

Another creepy note filled the screen.

This one said: NUMBER 8: CHOKING.

"The day after that, at the Hollywood Hilton, Ms. Sharp nearly choked to death on a small plastic key chain that had been cooked inside her morning omelette."

This time the camera was even shakier. An emergency team of medics swarmed around Vee Sharp, who lay on the floor of her hotel room. Her chest heaved up and down as she hacked and coughed.

"Whoa," I muttered under my breath. "That's intense."

The monitor went blank for a second. Then a bunch of publicity stills flashed across the screen, ending with a grainy black-and-white close-up of Vee's face.

"As you can imagine," the voice went on, *"Ms. Sharp's managers and producers are extremely concerned. Tomorrow the pop star will begin shooting her next music video on a Hollywood soundstage. Even though the studio has been thoroughly checked by security, everyone is worried that there could be more attacks."*

Frank shook his head. "Man, she must be freaking out."

I nodded in agreement.

The announcer started talking again. *"Ms. Sharp's agent has asked the FBI to send a pair of young agents to her video shoot . . . disguised as interns. The FBI turned to us. Joe and Frank Hardy, you're going to Hollywood."*

Wow. We're going to meet Vee Sharp!

Frank noticed the excitement in my eyes. "Calm down, Joe. You don't want to act like a drooling fan."

"Shut up," I said, smacking his arm.

I tried to concentrate on the computer screen. But my face was turning red. I could feel it.

"Our tech team has created a couple of new toys for you boys," the voice continued. *"The mini MP3 players can record and play music, of course. But they also can be used as walkie-talkies."*

I examined the small wireless devices. "Cool."

"The silver pen-shaped instrument is a new thermal tool we've developed," said the voice. *"It can instantly heat up and cut through hard surfaces such as glass and steel."*

On the screen, a pair of hands demonstrated the device, cutting through a thick windowpane in seconds.

"Awesome," I gasped.

"We'll send you a complete travel itinerary via e-mail," said the announcer. *"Joe, Frank . . . good luck. This CD will be reformatted in five seconds. Four. Three. Two. One."*

The computer screen went black. Music erupted through Frank's speakers.

It was Vee Sharp's brand-new hit song, "Girls Rule."

Playback flapped his wings and started squawking along with the rhythm.

"Girls rule! Girls rule!"

"I guess you aren't the only Vee Sharp fan," Frank pointed out.

I frowned. "Well, it looks like one of her fans wants her dead."

Frank stood up. "Come on. Let's go tell Mom and Dad. We're going to Hollywood!"

"You are *not* going to Hollywood," said Mom when we told her the news. "You just got back from New York."

"But Mom," I pleaded. "We'll get to be interns for Vee Sharp's video shoot. It's an amazing career opportunity."

Mom rolled her eyes. "So you want to be music video directors now? Last week you wanted to be race car drivers. And before that you wanted to be computer game designers."

"We're exploring our options," I said.

"Well, maybe you should explore your school-books. You're not doing so well in algebra, you know," said Mom, sitting up in her chair.

"But Mom," I said. "It's Vee Sharp."

"Didn't you just see her in concert?" Mom replied.

Frank stepped forward to explain—with a clever lie. "That's how we found out about the internship," he told her. "At the concert, they announced that they're having a contest. Joe and I filled out the entry forms . . . and we won! Millions of kids would kill for a chance to work with Vee Sharp."

Dad walked up behind Mom's chair and started massaging her neck. "Come on, honey," he crooned. "Let them do it. They won the contest. They can't turn it down."

Mom frowned. "What about Joe's algebra class?"

"I'll bet Joe will learn more during this video shoot than he will in algebra class."

Way to go, Dad!

Mom grimaced. "But who will go with them, Fenton?" she said to Dad. "We promised to help with the Policeman's Ball this week. And while I'd let the boys go just about anywhere on their own, interning for a rock star in Hollywood is something I feel needs a bit of supervision."

Just then Aunt Trudy strolled into the living room with a bag of chips and a bowl of homemade dip.

"I'll go," she volunteered.

We all looked up in surprise.

"I haven't been to Los Angeles in years," she told us. "It'll give me a chance to catch up with Betty Clark. I haven't seen her since high school. I've been meaning to visit her out there."

Aunt Trudy?

I mulled this over. It would be pretty bad having Trudy around while I was trying to make a good impression on Vee—but it might not be *so* bad. Besides, if this was the only way we'd be able to go . . .

Frank and I held our breath as Mom thought it over.

"Please," I said.

Finally she sighed and shrugged her shoulders. "Okay. You boys can go to Hollywood."

We both cheered, jumping up and high-fiving each other.

"All right!"

"But I'm warning you," Mom said, holding up a finger. "I don't want you two getting into any kind of trouble."

"We won't," I promised.

Yeah, right.

"And I want you to listen to your Aunt Trudy," she added. "Remember, she's in charge."

"Isn't she always?" Frank said with a wink.

Aunt Trudy flicked a potato chip at him and laughed.

My brother gave me a big thumbs-up.

"California, here we come!"

4.

Hooray for Hollywood

The cross-country plane ride seemed endless. Aunt Trudy snored through the entire trip. The baggage claim took forever. And the waiting line for a rental car seemed even longer than our flight.

But hey—we made it. We were in Los Angeles!

I smiled the whole way to our hotel in West Hollywood. The sun was shining, the wind was blowing in my hair, and even Aunt Trudy was grinning from ear to ear.

"This hotel has a pool, doesn't it?" she asked, adjusting her big, round sunglasses.

"Yup," I answered. "I checked out the hotel's Web site. It has a great pool with an outdoor bar and restaurant."

"Oh, good." Aunt Trudy rubbed her hands

28

together. "I can't wait to slip into my swimsuit, take a nice relaxing dip, and order one of those fancy fruity cocktails in a coconut shell."

"Aunt Trudy!" I said, a little surprised. "I thought *you* were supposed to keep an eye on *us*, not the other way around."

She waved me off. "Oh, don't worry, Frank. Your Aunt Trudy is the world's best chaperone."

I didn't like the sound of that.

And neither did Joe.

"Aunt Trudy," he said, "you know we're going to be *very* busy at the studio shooting this music video, right? I'm afraid if you tag along, it might be a little, um . . ."

"Embarrassing for you?" she asked. "Relax, boys. I've heard that those film sets can be awfully boring. I plan to catch up with my old friend Betty and do a little shopping and sightseeing."

Joe and I sighed with relief.

"Is that our hotel?" Aunt Trudy asked. She pointed to a pink and yellow two-story building with a turquoise pool in front.

"Yup," I said, steering the rental car into the parking lot.

"I hope they have pool boys," she said, "to wait on me hand and foot."

"Aunt Trudy!"

• • •

A half hour later, we were settled into our rooms. Joe and I didn't bother to unpack. We were anxious to head over to the studio and check out the music video shoot.

Aunt Trudy didn't want to waste any time either.

In a matter of minutes, she was kicking back in a lounge chair, wearing a swimsuit, a robe, sunglasses, and a big straw hat. A tall young man from the bar handed her a cocktail in a large coconut shell with a long pink straw and a little paper umbrella.

Joe and I waved to her as we walked past the pool toward the parking lot.

Aunt Trudy sipped her cocktail and waved back.

"Hooray for Hollywood!" she hooted.

The studio was only a fifteen-minute drive from our hotel. I had to admit I was excited. And the closer we got, the more excited I became.

We're in Hollywood! For a music video shoot! With Vee Sharp!

We drove up to the security gate, gave our names to the guard, and were immediately waved inside.

"Lot Five, Building A," the guard told us. "There's parking right outside the building."

I drove the rental car carefully past a row of large windowless warehouses. There were people everywhere: burly guys moving giant pieces of scenery, wardrobe people pushing racks full of clothes, movie extras dressed up in costumes from ancient Rome, the Old West, or Victorian England. There was even one guy in full Frankenstein makeup.

"How cool is this?" said Joe.

"Way cool," I replied.

I spotted a sign for Lot Five and steered the rental car through another gate.

"Here we are," I said. "Building A."

I stopped and parked. Joe hopped out of the car before I even managed to undo my seat belt.

"Okay, where is she?" he asked, eyes gleaming. "Where's Vee Sharp?"

"Easy, tiger," I said. "You don't want your girl-friend to think you're desperate."

"Look who's giving romance advice," he shot back. "You start stuttering if a girl just talks to you, Frank."

"Do not."

"Yeah, you do."

We walked to Building A and through a large double door. Inside, the place was huge. It reminded me of an airplane hangar—except the space was filled with large scenery panels, huge wooden boxes, metal scaffolding, and all sorts of lighting equipment.

A giant bear of a man in a flannel shirt stood in the middle of it all, waving his hands and ordering people around.

"You! Grab a couple of those scoop lights and take them to the spiderweb set! And you! We need more power cables!"

The man rubbed his bushy brown beard and watched his crew carry out his commands.

Finally his eyes landed on Joe and me.

"Who are you two?" he shouted across the soundstage.

My brother and I stepped forward.

"I'm Frank Hardy," I said, extending my hand. "And this is my brother Joe. We're the interns that Vee's agent requested."

The big man's eyes lit up.

"Great!" he said. "We could use a few more hands around here. I'm Brewster Fink, production manager."

He shook our hands so hard that it hurt.

"These music video shoots are always understaffed," he told us. "Not like the big Hollywood feature films. Those productions have huge crews. But for this, the budget is smaller. And I'll take all the help I can get. In fact, let me introduce you to someone."

Vee Sharp, maybe?

My heart started pounding when he waved at a girl standing behind a cluster of lights.

"Jillian! Come over here!"

The girl ducked under a scaffold and approached us. She wasn't Vee Sharp, but she was almost as pretty. With long strawberry blond hair and blue eyes, she even resembled Vee a little bit.

"Jillian, I'd like you to meet Frank and Joe Hardy," said Brewster. "They're the contest winners for the music video internship."

She looked at us and smiled. "Contest winners, huh?"

"Yeah, we're pretty psyched," said Joe.

Contest? ATAC's good.

Jillian shot a glance at Brewster. "Well, you guys might not be so psyched once Brewster starts barking orders at you."

Brewster burst out laughing.

"Jillian Goode is the president of the Vee Sharp Fan Club," he explained. "Vee invited her here to watch the video shoot, and I, well, I . . ."

"He snapped me up and put me to work."

Joe and I laughed.

"We don't mind a little work," I said.

"How about a *lot* of work?" said Jillian.

"Don't listen to her," Brewster told us. "She just wants to devote her life to being Vee Sharp's number one fan."

His words echoed in my head. *Vee Sharp's number one fan.*

I started thinking about the threatening letters the pop star had received. The first three of the "Top Ten Ways to Die" had been delivered with Vee's fan mail.

I studied Jillian Goode's face. She seemed harmless enough—young, pretty, enthusiastic—a typical teenage fan.

But sometimes fans can be a little crazy.

Crazy enough to kill?

A chill rushed through me.

I almost jumped when Brewster threw his arms around Joe and me. "Come on, boys. Let me give you a little tour."

The big bearded man led us toward the back of the building, pointing out large props and scenery that were still under construction.

"This is the scene we're shooting today," he told us. "The Black Widow's Web."

I looked up and whistled.

Huge black-and-white panels towered overhead, each painted with long swooping strands of a giant spiderweb. The webbing was cut out in a series of frames to give the illusion of depth. It looked like a cartoon come to life.

"That's totally awesome," said Joe.

"I wish everybody thought so," Brewster muttered.

"What do you mean?"

"Mr. Hotshot Director, Spider Jones, wasn't happy with it," he explained. "We're still making changes."

"Spider Jones?" I said. "*The* Spider Jones?"

Brewster nodded grimly.

I was blown away. Spider Jones was the hottest director working in music videos. All the biggest stars used him—from Madonna to Britney Spears to Green Day. His videos were legendary.

"Speak of the devil," said Brewster, staring over my shoulder.

I turned around to see the famous Spider Jones marching toward us. He looked just like his pictures in the magazines—tall, lean, and lanky, with wraparound shades and spiky black hair.

But he didn't look very happy.

"No, no, NO, Brewster!" he yelled. "I asked for *less*, not *more*! There are too many panels here! It's *much* too cluttered! I said *simple*, Brewster! Can you say *simple*?"

"Simple," Brewster repeated, rolling his eyes.

"Yes, *simple*. And *flat*. Like a *cartoon*," said the director, emphasizing each word with a jab of his finger.

Joe nudged me. "It looks like a cartoon to me," he whispered.

Spider Jones spun around and glared at us. "And *who* are *you*?"

Oh, no.

Joe bit his lip.

Brewster stepped in to introduce us. "These are the new interns, Spider," he said. "Frank and Joe Hardy."

"Ah, interns," the director sneered. "*Not* art directors. Just *fix* the set, Brewster! Make some of those panels *go away*!"

Then Spider spun around and marched off.

Brewster looked at us and sighed.

"Terrific," said Joe. "The world's greatest video director hates me."

"Don't worry about it," Brewster assured him. "By tomorrow, Spider won't even remember meeting you. He's way too focused on the *sets*. And the *star*."

He jabbed his finger at us and laughed.

"Speaking of the *star*," I said, "where *is* Ms. Sharp?"

"In her Mansion on Wheels."

"Mansion on Wheels?"

Brewster waved us toward the back of the set. A barn-sized doorway led outside to a row of parked trailers. One of them was easily twice the size of the others. Long, tall, and supersleek, the deluxe mobile home even had big bay windows and a small porch with columns.

"That's Ms. Sharp's private trailer," said Brewster.

"That's a trailer?" asked Joe. "I've never seen a trailer like that before."

"You should see inside. It's like a mini spa, complete with massage table, tanning booth, and Jacuzzi."

"Jacuzzi?" said Joe. "Sweet."

Brewster turned back to his crew. "Hey, guys!" he shouted. "We need to remove the second and third panels!"

He walked off and left Joe and me standing there, staring at Vee Sharp's trailer.

"Impressive, huh?" I said to my brother.

Joe nodded slowly. "You know what the coolest thing is about that trailer?"

"What?"

"Vee Sharp is inside of it. *Vee Sharp!* Can you believe it, Frank?"

I started to say something, but Joe hushed me. "Shhh. Listen."

In spite of the crew moving panels behind us, I

could hear the faint sound of music coming from inside the trailer. I recognized the song right away.

It was Vee Sharp's newest hit single, "Girls Rule."

And Vee Sharp herself was singing along with it!

"Listen to that, Frank!" said Joe, mesmerized. "Listen to her voice! She's really good. No, she's better than that—she's great. She's—"

Screaming.

Vee Sharp was definitely screaming.

"HELP! HELP! SOMEBODY, HELP!"

5.

Spider Attack!

I heard another scream from inside the trailer.

"HELP ME!"

Without even thinking, I dashed toward the trailer and ripped open the door. Frank was right behind me. We scrambled up the steps—and froze.

There she was.

Vee Sharp.

One of the most famous pop stars in the world.

Covered with spiders.

"Help me, please," she whispered, looking at us with absolute terror in her famous blue eyes.

She sat back on a white leather lounge chair, her long blond hair streaming over her shoulders. She was wearing a black latex jumpsuit—probably for

39

the Black Widow scene—and her body was covered with big, fat, hairy spiders.

Tarantulas.

"Okay, don't move," I said in a low voice. "We'll get them off of you. Don't worry."

She looked me in the eye and pursed her lips. I almost felt like fainting.

It's Vee Sharp! In the flesh!

I tried not to be starstruck. Instead I turned my attention to the furry tarantulas crawling across her jumpsuit. There must have been six or seven of them—at least.

"They won't bite if you don't scare them," I told Vee.

"That's comforting," she said with just a trace of sarcasm in her voice.

"Joe, look," said my brother. "Under the chair."

He picked up a plastic-coated shoebox from the floor. There was a label on it with the word TARANTULAS written in magic marker. Inside the box was a small note.

It was another threat—a new entry in the "Top Ten Ways to Die." Each letter had been cut and pasted from magazine headlines.

"'Number Seven: Spider bites,'" Frank whispered.

Vee let out a little whimper.

"Okay, just relax," I said.

Vee sucked in her breath. I reached for a tarantula on her left arm. The creature wriggled its legs as I picked it up gently between my thumb and forefinger. Frank held up the box. I dropped the spider inside.

"There you go," I said softly.

I plucked another tarantula off her shoulder while Frank scooped up a third one on her knee.

"See? No problem," I said to Vee.

She tried to smile.

Then another spider started crawling up her neck.

"*Ewwwww*. Yuck . . ."

I slipped my hand against her collarbone and slid my fingers beneath the tarantula's hairy legs. Vee shuddered. As I dropped it into the box, Frank found another one scuttling up her black leather boot.

"Don't move," he said. "I got it."

He picked up the spider and placed it carefully in the box with the others. I thought we had them all, but then I spotted two more—one on her thigh and another on her stomach.

"Okay, just a couple more," I told Vee.

The pop star took a deep breath.

Frank grabbed the spider on her leg while I went after the one on her stomach. Unfortunately, the furry creature didn't like the looks of my hand coming toward it. The tarantula scrambled across her hip and disappeared into the chair.

"Okay," I said. "On the count of three, I want you to stand up. Very slowly."

Vee nodded.

"One. Two. Three."

She stood up. The tarantula slipped off her back and landed on the seat of the chair. Frank snatched it up and plopped it into the box.

"Is it gone?" Vee asked, gasping.

"Yes," I said. "But turn around slowly . . . so we can make sure."

Vee cleared her throat, lifted her arms, and rotated slowly.

"Joe, look," said my brother.

"What is it?" said Vee, her voice tightening.

"Don't move," I told her. "There's just one more."

"Where is it?"

"In your hair."

"Gross!"

I had to admit it *was* gross. An extra-large tarantula was tangled up in the long blond strands that flowed down Vee's back. I tried to untangle it—but the creepy crawler was stubborn. It didn't want to leave its new home.

"Hold on, hold on," I mumbled as I lifted up her hair and shook it gently.

Frank held the box underneath. After a little coaxing, the spider wriggled free and fell.

"Got it!" said Frank, stepping back with the box. He examined the spiders before fastening the lid. "Let's see. We've got . . . five, six, seven tarantulas here."

"And one person who wants to kill me," Vee added.

I glanced at Frank.

"So who are you guys?" she asked.

"I'm Joe Hardy," I said, shaking her hand. "And this is my brother Frank. We're interns for the video shoot. This is our first day."

She collapsed into the lounge chair and sighed. "Welcome to my life," she mumbled. "And maybe my death, too."

"What do you mean?" said Frank.

Vee offered us a seat on the big overstuffed sofa. Like the lounge chair, it was white leather and looked incredibly expensive.

Vee took a breath and folded her arms over her chest. "It's not easy being a star. I mean, sure, there's the glamour and the fame and the big fancy private trailer."

She waved her hands at the plush interior of

her Mansion on Wheels. Brewster Fink was right. The place was amazing. Filled with ultra-modern chrome lamps, polished wood cabinets, and white fur pillows, it looked like something out of a magazine.

"But it's hard when you reach the top," Vee went on. "Everybody wants to drag you down. Or worse."

She turned, opened a cabinet, and pulled out a few pieces of paper. She handed them to me. But I didn't have to look at them to know what they were.

They were the death threats we had seen on the ATAC CD.

Top Ten Ways to Die.

I showed them to Frank, who pretended he was seeing them for the first time.

"Who would want to do this to you?" he asked.

Vee closed her eyes and bit her lip. "I don't know. Anyone. Everyone. Sometimes I think the whole world is against me. The magazines gossip about me. Comedians tell jokes about me. I'm like one big singing and dancing target."

There was a knock at the door.

"Come in!"

The door opened, and a short guy with long braids and a purple sweat suit stepped inside.

"Vee? Are you okay?" he asked in a high, squeaky voice. "I thought I heard you scream."

"Yes, T-Mix, I'm fine," she answered. "Just a little, um, wardrobe malfunction."

T-Mix frowned, then laughed.

"T-Mix, I'd like you to meet Joe and Frank Hardy," Vee said. "They're the interns."

T-Mix nodded his head and made a peace sign with his fingers.

I didn't know what to say. It was T-Mix! The man! The myth!

T-Mix was the most sought-after record producer in the industry. He could take anybody, regardless of talent or ability, and squeeze a Top Ten hit out of them. He was a total legend. The mastermind behind the biggest bands of all time.

I tried to muster up the courage to say something like, "Dude! You're the man!"

But I never got the chance.

The high-strung director, Spider Jones, stormed into the trailer like a human tornado.

"VEE! My *star*!" he screeched. "Did I hear you *scream*? What's *wrong*, my *darling*?"

Vee sighed. "I'm okay, Spider. Relax."

Asking Spider to relax was like asking a fish to skateboard—it wasn't going to happen.

Vee pointed to the box of spiders on Frank's lap. "Somebody put tarantulas in my trailer," she told the director.

Spider Jones gasped, then ripped the wrap-around shades off his face—and exploded.

"*How* did this happen? *Who* is responsible? This is *unacceptable*!"

He stuck his head out of the trailer door and continued screaming.

"BRING ME THE ANIMAL WRANGLER! *Now!*"

Ranting and raving, he marched off toward the soundstage.

I looked at Vee, who didn't seem surprised by the director's behavior. "Wow," I said. "At least he seems concerned for your welfare."

Vee scoffed. "Are you kidding? He only cares about his precious *art*. He's afraid this will ruin his video shoot."

"But you're the star," I pointed out.

"As far as *he* is concerned, Spider Jones is the star. The man hates my guts."

Frank shot me a glance, then leaned forward. "Why do you say that?"

She sat back in her chair. "At first I refused to work with live spiders in the video. But Spider insisted. He uses spiders in all of his videos. It's his trademark."

What an ego.

"Finally I agreed to do it," she continued. "But

SUSPECT PROFILE

Name: Jonathon Jones, aka "Spider"

Hometown: Seattle, Washington

Physical description: 25 years old, 6'1", 150 lbs., black spiky hair, brown eyes, wears wraparound sunglasses and vintage leisure suits from the 1970s.

Occupation: Music video director, VTV Award winner

Background: Raised in a trailer park, resented the rich kids at school, moved to Los Angeles to find fame and fortune, talked his way onto a TV commercial set, "borrowed" the camera to make his own video—which he used to land his first big job, pushed hard to get to the top.

Suspicious behavior: Insisted on using deadly spiders in the video shoot, badmouthed Vee Sharp, made threats to the crew.

Suspected of: Sending death threats to Vee Sharp and endangering her life.

Possible motives: Jealousy, competition, mental breakdown.

then, this morning I overheard Spider complaining about me to the entire crew. He called me a 'spoiled no-talent brat.'"

"That creep," I muttered. "He's just jealous that you're more famous than he is."

"Maybe," Vee said with a sigh. "But that's no excuse for what he said next. He told the crew that he would kill me if I ruined his video."

I looked at Frank—and I knew exactly what he was thinking.

We have our first suspect.

6.

Sink or Swim

The next morning, Joe and I woke up early to take advantage of the free Continental breakfast by the pool. Unfortunately, we didn't make it in time.

"All the good stuff is gone," Joe whined, staring down at the buffet.

He was right. All that was left was a brown banana and two tiny oranges. No donuts, no Danishes, no muffins.

"Good morning, sleepyheads!"

It was Aunt Trudy—floating on an inflatable raft in the middle of the pool. She held a cup of coffee in one hand and a plate of pastries in the other.

"Aunt Trudy," I said. "You grabbed all the goodies."

"Well, you know what they say. The early bird catches the cinnamon bun," she said, winking. "Actually, I was saving them for you boys."

She paddled her way to the edge of the pool and handed me the plate. Joe grabbed an apple tart and sank his teeth in.

"What time did you boys get back last night?" Aunt Trudy asked. "I was waiting up for you, but I needed my beauty rest."

What had gotten into Aunt Trudy? I hadn't seen her this cheery in years!

"We were shooting until ten o'clock," I said. "The crew had to make last-minute changes on the set. They built this big spiderweb, and Vee Sharp was dressed up as a black widow."

Aunt Trudy grunted. "Now why would they make such a pretty girl dress up like a spider?"

"Her song is called 'Girls Rule,'" I explained. "It's all about strong women, so the director wants to showcase Vee in a bunch of different roles. Last night she was a black widow and they filmed her with live tarantulas."

Aunt Trudy made a face. "Poor girl. That must have been awful for her."

Joe shook his head. "No, she was a real trouper, Aunt Trudy. You should have seen how brave she was."

A smile crept over Aunt Trudy's face. "I think Vee Sharp has a secret admirer."

"Not so secret," I said with a laugh. "You should have seen them making eyes at each other. I think they're in love."

Joe almost choked on his apple tart. "Look who's talking, Frank! You spent half the night flirting with Jillian Goode!"

"Who's Jillian Goode?" asked Aunt Trudy.

"The president of the Vee Sharp Fan Club," said Joe. "She's got a huge crush on Frank."

"No, she doesn't," I said.

"Yes, she does."

I threw a donut at him.

"Hey!" snapped Aunt Trudy. "Don't waste the food! This hotel is a little stingy with their Continental breakfast. And I need my energy today. I'm meeting my friend Betty. We're going to take one of those bus tours of celebrity homes."

I was relieved that Aunt Trudy was keeping herself busy.

"That's cool. Have fun with Betty. And say hello for us." I stood up and pulled the car keys out of my pocket. "Come on, Joe. We have to get going now. I have a feeling we have another killer day ahead of us."

• • •

When we pulled into the studio lot, we were surprised to see a flatbed truck with a large water tank parked in front of Building A.

"I wonder what this is all about," I said, getting out of the rental car.

"There's one way to find out," said Joe, pointing to the ground. "Follow the hose."

A big black rubber hose led from the tank into the building, uncoiling across the soundstage like a giant snake in a horror film. Finally we reached the end.

"Wow," said Joe. "Check it out."

A gigantic larger-than-life goldfish bowl sat on an oversized nightstand next to a humongous bed. The whole set looked like a boy's bedroom—but built in monster scale.

"What do you think?"

Brewster Fink came up behind us, beaming with pride.

"It's awesome," I said.

"The crew worked on it all night long," he told us. "But that's not all. Come take a look at this."

Brewster led around the set and pointed to another set. It was an exact replica of the giant bedroom—except human-size.

"We need to shoot the scene twice, in two different scales," the beard man explained. "Then we'll edit them together in postproduction. It's a special effect."

I didn't quite understand.

Brewster continued. "We'll shoot Vee Sharp inside the big goldfish bowl. Then we'll film a boy lying in the smaller bed watching the bowl. It'll look like the boy is staring at Vee in the bowl."

"Who's the boy?" Joe asked.

"You are," said Brewster.

"Me?"

"Yes, you. Spider says you have the look he wants for the scene. Will you do it?"

"Um, well, ah, sure, okay," Joe sputtered.

I gave him a little kick in the shin.

"Break a leg, Joe," I teased.

Brewster laughed. Suddenly Spider Jones dashed onto the set.

"*You!* Intern!" spouted the director, pointing at Joe. "Go to the wardrobe trailer and get into your pajamas! *Now!* And where's my *star*? Somebody bring Vee to the set!"

Jillian Goode rounded the corner, pushing an empty wheelchair. "I'll get her, Mr. Jones!" she said.

Why does Vee Sharp need a wheelchair? I wondered. *Has she been injured? Or attacked?*

Joe and I ran after Jillian. "Wait!" I shouted. "Jillian!"

She stopped in front of Vee's trailer.

"Is Vee okay?" said Joe, his face filled with concern. "What's up with the wheelchair?"

Jillian giggled. "Vee can't walk in her mermaid costume."

"Mermaid costume?"

Joe's eyes lit up—and I started laughing.

"Control yourself, bro," I whispered in his ear. "Go get into your pajamas. And get ready for your close-up."

I pushed him toward the wardrobe trailer.

A few minutes later, Joe was ready to go. I had to laugh at the powder blue pajamas they made him wear. Covered with little stars and moons, they looked like something a five-year-old would wear.

But they weren't as funny as his makeup.

"*Awww*, Joe! You look so *cute*!" I teased.

My brother rolled his eyes—which only made him look funnier. The makeup artist had put rosy pink circles on his cheeks and long brown lashes on his eyelids. He looked like a little boy in a comic book.

"Places, everyone! *PLACES!*"

Spider Jones clapped his hands, and the entire

crew jumped into action. Joe quickly hopped into bed, resting his head on the big fluffy pillow.

The tall, thin director crouched down in front of him.

"Now listen, Joe," he explained softly. "You're a little boy, and it's bedtime. But you can't stop looking at your goldfish bowl. Why? Because your favorite fish has miraculously turned into a beautiful mermaid."

Joe frowned thoughtfully and nodded his head.

"Okay! *LIGHTS! CAMERA!*"

Spider stood up and positioned himself behind the cameraman. He pointed a finger at my brother, who glanced around the set nervously.

Poor Joe. He looked terrified.

"*ACTION!*"

The camera started whirring. Joe turned his head slowly on the pillow and gazed at the goldfish bowl on the nightstand.

"*CUT!*"

The cameraman stopped filming. Spider Jones jumped like a jackrabbit, waving his hands in front of Joe's face.

"No, no, *NO!*" he shouted. "I want to see *love*. I want to see *mystery*. I want to see *passion*."

Joe bit his lip.

"No, no, *NO*," Spider squealed, throwing his

hands into the air. "Perhaps you need some inspiration, John."

"Joe," my brother corrected him.

"Whatever," said Spider, spinning around toward the crew. "Where is my *star*? Bring in *Ms. Sharp*!"

"I'll get her, sir," said Jillian Goode.

The young fan club president disappeared around the corner and returned a few seconds later with Vee Sharp in the wheelchair.

"Wow," I muttered under my breath.

Vee Sharp made a beautiful mermaid. Her long, flowing hair was decorated with small seashells, and her shiny green tail fin flopped gracefully over the edge of the wheelchair.

The whole crew burst into applause.

"Magnificent," said Spider Jones. He pushed Jillian aside and wheeled the stunning pop star onto the small bedroom set. "We'll place you right here, Ms. Sharp," he said, positioning her behind the nightstand. "Now Jack here can see what he's looking at."

"It's *Joe*," my brother and Vee corrected the director at the same time. Then their eyes met, and they both started giggling.

"Quiet, please," said Spider. "*Quiet* on the set! Lights, camera, *ACTION*!"

Joe laid his head on the pillow. Then, slowly

turning, he stared at the goldfish bowl—and at Vee.

"That's it, Joe," the director whispered. "You're looking at a *beautiful* mermaid. Yes, yes. You *love* her, Joe. You want to *kiss* her, Joe."

My brother started blushing.

"*Excellent*, Joe," Spider gasped. "That's it. Keep *staring*. Yes! And *CUT*!"

Jillian Goode snuck up next to me. "Your brother and Vee seem to have good chemistry together," she whispered.

I had to admit she was right. My brother, the ladies' man.

After a few more takes, the crew moved the camera and some lights to the giant-size bedroom set. Jillian wheeled Vee Sharp next to the enormous nightstand, where Brewster Fink was ready to hook the star up to a tall crane.

"We're going to lower you into the water very slowly," he explained to Vee. "Are you going to be all right?"

Vee nodded. "Sure. This will be fun. And don't worry. I'm a good swimmer."

Joe came up beside me, wiping the makeup off his face with a large towel. "I don't like the looks of this," he said. "Vee could get hurt."

He was right.

The goldfish bowl was about ten feet tall and ten

feet across. Filled with water, it must have weighed a ton. I sure hoped the giant nightstand was strong enough to support it.

We moved in closer for a better view.

Brewster Fink placed a harness around Vee's shoulders. Then he hooked her up to a cable that was connected to the crane. Spider Jones walked onto the set, smiled at his star, and started talking about the scene. The cameraman and crew finished setting up.

"We're ready to go, Spider," said Brewster.

The director stood up and clapped his hands. "Okay! *Quiet* on the set! Get Ms. Sharp into position!"

Brewster waved at the crane operator, who pulled a lever, and the sound of a motor echoed inside the building. Slowly, Vee Sharp was lifted up, higher and higher—until she was dangling in the air over the goldfish bowl.

"Hello, down there!" she shouted out, flapping and waving her mermaid's tail at us.

We laughed and waved back.

"Okay! Lower her into the bowl!" Brewster shouted.

Down, down, down she went—her tail fin plunging into the water.

"Okay, stop!"

Brewster climbed up a tall steel ladder and

unhooked the harness from Vee's shoulders. With a splash, she fell into the water. Completely immersed, her long hair flowing around her, she swam back and forth like a fish. Finally her head popped up on the surface.

"How's that, Spider?" she asked.

"Perfect! *Perfect!*" he cheered. "Do it just like that for the camera. And don't forget to *beckon* with your arms."

Brewster folded up the ladder and carried it off the set. "Move the crane back!" he yelled. "It's casting a shadow."

Soon everything was ready to go. Spider Jones asked everyone to be quiet, and the cameras started rolling.

"*ACTION!*"

Vee Sharp started swimming back and forth in the goldfish bowl. She waved her tail fin and beckoned with her arms.

So far, so good.

Then I heard a strange sound—like wire snapping.

I tilted my head and looked upward. Something dangled in the air above the entire set. A pair of cables had broken.

And a whole section of the bedroom wall was falling.

"Look out!" I yelled.

But it was too late. A tall panel tilted forward and landed on top of the goldfish bowl. The whole soundstage trembled. Vee Sharp looked up and panicked. Air bubbled out of her mouth as she swam upward, beating her hands against the panel. But it wouldn't budge.

Vee Sharp was trapped.

And drowning.

7.

Girl Under Glass

Jillian Goode screamed. "She's going to drown! Somebody do something!"

Brewster Fink and his crew rushed onto the set, grabbing the fallen panel and trying to lift it off.

"Come on! Lift!" he shouted.

But it was useless. The giant panel was wedged against the rest of the scenery.

Vee!

I stared helplessly into the fishbowl. Vee struggled and thrashed underwater, her fists pounding against the thick glass.

I had to think fast.

The panel was stuck on top of the bowl. I glanced across the set and spotted a large sledgehammer on the floor. Maybe I could smash through the glass.

No. Vee could get hurt.

Jillian jumped up and down, still screaming. Spider Jones waved his arms wildly in the air. Everyone was rushing around in a panic . . . but doing nothing to save her.

Then Brewster had an idea. "Bring the crane over!" he yelled. "We can lift the panel off."

The crane operator jumped behind the controls—but I knew he wouldn't be able to make it in time.

Vee's drowning!

Her body twisted and turned frantically in the water. Swimming forward, she tried kicking against the glass with her tail fin. But it was no use.

Suddenly her whole body buckled. I watched in horror as a rush of air bubbles spewed from her mouth.

She's swallowing water!

I had to do something. Fast.

Then it hit me.

"Frank! Do you have the pocket pen?"

Before my brother could even answer me, I thrust my hand into his jacket and pulled out the small silver device we had received from ATAC.

The thermal cutting tool.

I dashed across the set and climbed up onto the oversized nightstand.

"Get back, Vee! Move away from the glass!" I shouted, waving my hand at her.

She seemed to understand. Once she swam to the far end of the fishbowl, I charged up the small tool with a push of a button. Then I pressed it against the glass.

First the tip turned red. A thin stream of smoke drifted up from the glass.

It's working!

I pressed harder and harder, and soon the tip of the device started pushing through the glass. Inch after inch, it melted a narrow groove on the surface. Guiding it along, I carved a large circle into the side of the bowl. Water sprayed, then gushed, across my hand.

Yes!

Suddenly the circle broke away, grazing my shoulder as it flew to the ground. A heavy flow of cold water splashed across my face—and the water level started falling.

I stood back and peered into the goldfish bowl. Vee floated faceup along the surface. Gasping for breath, she lifted her mouth up to the small pocket of air between the water and the panel.

"She's breathing!" Jillian shouted.

The crew started cheering.

"Come on, move this panel!" Brewster shouted to his crew. "Hook it onto the crane! Hurry!"

Inside the goldfish bowl, Vee Sharp coughed—and smiled.

It took another twenty minutes before they were able to pull Vee out of the water. Jillian waited on the sidelines with a big fluffy bathrobe, which she threw over Vee as soon as they lowered her into the wheelchair.

Vee was shaking. Her lip quivering, she looked up at me with a little smile and whispered, "Thank you, Joe."

"Anytime."

"Just one question. What did you use to cut through the glass?"

I wasn't about to tell her that I owned the latest top secret spy tool, so I said, "It's just something I ordered out of a catalogue."

That seemed to satisfy her. I had started to wheel her back to the trailer, when we heard a loud thud and the sound of gasps. I spun around to see what was going on.

The crane operator had lowered the fallen panel to the floor. Brewster Fink and the rest of the crew gathered around it, staring down in shock.

Large letters had been cut out and pasted on the back of the scenery: NUMBER 6: DROWNING.

Vee Sharp shivered.

"Come on," I said, pushing the wheelchair away. "Let's get you warmed up, Vee."

Frank, Jillian, and I wheeled the pop star to her trailer. Her long mermaid tail dragged on the ground beside her. We had to form a cradle with our arms to lift her up and carry her inside.

Finally we dropped her into the lounge chair, and Vee let out a loud sigh. "Top Ten Ways to Die," she mumbled.

Jillian looked confused, so Vee explained the whole story to her. Jillian listened carefully, then stood up.

"I think I know who's behind this," she said.

We all looked at her.

"Brewster Fink," she said.

Vee shook her head. "Brewster? No way."

Jillian started pacing back and forth. "Think about it. He has full access to all the props and sets. He's always the last one to leave the soundstage at the end of the day. And he certainly would know how to rig up the scenery to fall like that."

I glanced at Frank.

She had a point.

But Vee wasn't buying it. "It doesn't make any

sense. Why would Brewster want to hurt me?"

"Don't you remember? You threatened to fire him last summer," said Jillian. She looked at Frank and me. "Brewster messed up—big-time—during Vee's concert tour. He forgot to set up her key lights. She did half the show in total darkness."

"Brewster is part of your road crew?" I asked Vee.

Vee nodded. "Yeah. I use him all the time. He's an amazing technician. He can do anything: lights, sets, special effects, you name it. But that night, I guess I flipped out. I was so mad, I told him that I'd fire him if he screwed up again."

I thought about what she was saying.

Brewster Fink was there with Vee when she started receiving the Top Ten death threats.

Sure, Brewster *seemed* like a nice guy. But then I remembered the way he hollered at his crew.

"I still can't believe it's Brewster," Vee insisted. "We settled our problems long ago. We get along great now. He's just a big, sweet teddy bear."

"Well, maybe," said Jillian. "But who else could be doing this, Vee?"

The pop star shrugged. "I don't know. Maybe a crazed fan."

Jillian's face dropped.

She *was* the president of Vee's fan club, after all.

"I'm sorry! Not *you*, Jillian," said Vee, catching

herself. "You're great! I think of you more as a friend than a fan. I *totally* trust you."

Jillian looked up. "You do?"

"Completely. In fact, you're the only person I trust to help me get out of this stupid mermaid outfit."

She looked up at Frank and me and cleared her throat.

"Do you mind, boys?"

That was our cue to leave. So we left the trailer and headed back to the soundstage. On the way, we ran into T-Mix—the little producer with the huge talent.

"How's Vee?" he asked. "I just heard what happened."

We told T-Mix that his latest recording star was a little shaky, but okay.

He ran his hand through his long braids. "I guess it's not a good time to talk to Vee about doing a dance remix," he said. "'Girls Rule' is climbing up the charts. We should release a new version for the clubs."

I looked at T-Mix. "I'm not sure if it's a good time to drag Vee back into a studio right now. But I guess it can't hurt to ask."

T-Mix thought about it. "Maybe I'll ask her after lunch."

He turned around and walked away. Frank and I

crossed the soundstage, heading back to the scene of the crime. The crew was busy knocking down the set and stacking the panels against the wall.

We looked around for Brewster. We wanted to ask him if there was something we could do to help out. We found him in the corner, talking to Spider Jones.

The director waved his arms at Brewster. "*How? How* did this happen? *Who* hung the scenery panel? *Who?*"

Brewster lowered his head. "I did, sir."

Spider freaked out. "*You? You* are responsible? *You* almost killed *my star*!"

Brewster looked up. "I don't understand it. I checked and double-checked the rigging. Everything was secure. I don't understand how this happened."

Spider folded his long arms across his narrow chest. "I don't know what to say, Brewster. Maybe you should *triple*-check *everything* from now on. *Vee Sharp was almost killed.*"

Brewster didn't say anything.

"Vee Sharp is a *huge star*. She's one of the most *powerful* young women in show business! If you mess up this video shoot, Brewster, *you'll never work in this town again*!"

The director spun around and stalked off.

SUSPECT PROFILE

Name: Brewster Fink

Hometown: Moose Gulch, South Dakota

Physical description: 37 years old, 6'5", 245 lbs., husky build, brown wavy hair, beard, green eyes, wears flannel shirts and jeans.

Occupation: Production manager for video and film, Vee Sharp's road crew manager

Background: Self-made carpenter and electrician, left home to pursue acting but had no success, forced to join production crews and work behind the scenes.

Suspicious behavior: Has a short temper and a violent streak, confessed to rigging up the scenery that almost killed Vee Sharp.

Suspected of: Threatening Vee Sharp and attempted homicide.

Possible motives: Professional jealousy, personal dispute, private grudge.

Brewster just stood there, breathing in and out slowly.

I felt terrible for the guy.

But maybe I shouldn't have.

Maybe Brewster was guilty.

Frank and I waited a few minutes before approaching him. Then we asked Brewster if there was anything we could do.

He glanced up at us with a strange look on his face. He blinked his eyes, rubbed his beard, and cleared his throat. "Yeah, sure," he said softly. "You can help the crew stack up the panels. Thanks, boys."

He turned and walked away.

As he rounded the corner, he let out a loud grunt.

Then he swung his fist through the air. And knocked over a ladder.

"Did you see that?" Frank whispered.

"Yes, I did," I said.

Frank frowned. "It looks like the big, sweet teddy bear has a big, bad temper."

The director clapped his hands sharply. "Places, everyone! *Where is my star?*"

Jillian Goode popped her head around the backdrop of stars. "Vee's on her way, but she's moving a little slow!"

We all looked up and waited. Finally, Vee came lumbering around the corner in a huge bulky spacesuit. The crew started laughing and applauding.

Vee tried to take a bow—but it was impossible for her to bend at the waist.

"Wow! Vee!" Spider gushed. "You look very . . . *authentic*! Take your place on the moon set, please."

"And be careful of the craters!" Brewster added with a worried look on his face.

Maybe Brewster is *innocent*, I thought. He seemed genuinely concerned about Vee's safety. In fact, he held her arm as she stepped onto the sand. Then, handing her the "Girls Rule" flag, he warned her once again about the plaster craters.

"Okay, OKAY!" Spider shouted, clapping his hands. "*Quiet* on the set! Vee, let's do a quick run-through before we shoot it. Remember: You're on the *moon*! There's very little *gravity*! You *bounce*! You *float*! Got it?"

Vee fastened the helmet over her head and nodded.

"Okay," said the director. "Ready? *Go!*"

"STOP!"

A deep voice bellowed from the other end of the soundstage. Everybody stopped and turned around.

"Stop shooting! We're closing down the production!"

A pot-bellied man stormed onto the set. With his jet black toupee, trimmed mustache, and shiny blue suit, he looked like a sleazy used-car salesman.

"Who's that?" I whispered to Jillian Goode.

"It's Jackson Puck," she said. "Vee's agent."

Following behind him was a young girl I recognized immediately. It was Vee Sharp's little sister, Kay. I'd seen her on one of those VTV reality shows, trying to launch a music career of her own. She came off like a total brat, bad-mouthing her famous big sister every chance she got. She even dyed her blond hair black so fans wouldn't confuse them.

"That's Kay Sharp, Vee's wicked half sister," whispered Jillian. She reached up and held her nose.

"You don't seem to like her very much," I said.

"Have you heard her sing?"

I nodded. "She doesn't have much talent, does she?"

"No, but she has an agent. Vee's agent."

I looked up and watched Jackson Puck. The

greasy-haired agent marched across the set and held his hand over the camera lens.

"I will *not* risk the safety of my client," he told Spider Jones. "Someone is threatening her life. There have already been a couple of attempts right here on this set."

Spider Jones stood up. "Calm down, Mr. Puck. We're taking every precaution to make sure Vee is safe."

"She almost drowned this morning!"

"But she's fine now! She *agreed* to continue shooting! We have a *schedule*!"

"And I have a *client* to protect." Jackson turned around and pointed at Vee. "Honey, go back to your trailer. You're done shooting for today."

Vee's face dropped. She started to protest, but Jackson waved his finger at her.

"Please, Vee. Go back to your trailer. I need to talk to the director . . . alone."

Vee sighed and lumbered her way across the moon set. Jillian took her arm and helped her. Meanwhile, Jackson Puck threw his arm around Spider Jones and started talking softly. They walked away so no one could hear them.

"I wish I knew what they were saying," I whispered to Joe.

Joe stared across the soundstage and squinted his eyes. His face lit up. "Do you have your MP3 player with you? The one that doubles as a walkie-talkie?"

I reached into my pocket and pulled it out. "Yes, but what's your point?"

"Look over there. See my jacket on the chair? My MP3 player is in the pocket."

Good thinking, Joe.

The director and the agent were just a few feet away from Joe's jacket. I popped one of the wireless headphones into my ear, handed Joe the other one, and adjusted my player. After a second or two of static, we were able to hear voices.

"But we have a contract."

"And I have a video to make."

"Vee is in danger."

Suddenly the voices faded. I looked up to see the two men stroll away—out of the player's hearing range. I glanced at Joe, who looked as disappointed as I was. We were about to pull the earphones out when another voice caught our attention.

"I am *so* sick of everyone making such a fuss over her."

Joe and I peered across the soundstage. Vee's sister Kay was leaning against the chair with Joe's jacket on it. She was talking into her cell phone— and we could hear every word she said.

"Jackson is supposed to be *my* agent too. But how can he launch *my* singing career when he's devoting all his time and energy to *her*? 'Little Miss Pop Star.' *Give me a break.*"

Joe shot me a look. "What a backstabber," he muttered.

"You of all people should understand where she's coming from, Joe. It must be hard to have an older, more talented sibling." I nudged his arm.

"Dream on, bro."

We both started to chuckle. But then Kay Sharp said something that chilled us to the bone.

"I just wish Vee would hurry up and *die* already."

Whoa.

Hearing that, we realized that Kay wasn't just a jealous little sister. She was a suspect.

Joe and I decided we'd better go check on Vee, so we walked across the soundstage and headed for her trailer. Before we even knocked, we could hear Vee's voice.

"What's that funny smell? Is it gas?"

I glanced at my brother, who pounded his fist on the door. "Vee? Vee! It's Joe!"

"Come in!"

We burst into the trailer. Vee Sharp stood in the middle of the room next to Jillian Goode. Their bodies were tensed up, their eyes scanning the room.

"Vee thinks she smells gas," said Jillian.

I held up a finger. "Nobody move. Just listen."

Everybody froze.

At first we couldn't hear anthing. Then a soft, whispery sound grabbed our attention. Slowly we turned toward the small kitchenette in the corner.

The stove was hissing.

The trailer was filling with gas!

9.

Night Stalkers

I took a step toward the hissing stove.

"Wait," said Frank. "Vee and Jillian, go outside. But open the door *slowly*. You don't want to set off any sparks."

The two girls inched their way to the trailer door, opened it carefully, and stepped outside.

"Joe, see if you can find the valve. I'll start opening windows."

My brother leaned toward the window behind the leather lounge chair, while I stooped down in front of the small stove.

"The pilot light is out," I said, examining the stovetop. I reached for the cabinet below and carefully opened the door. "I found the valve."

And that wasn't all.

There was another threat taped to the copper pipe: NUMBER 5: GAS.

I reached in and grasped the valve. After a few turns, the stove stopped hissing. "There. It's off."

Frank let out of sigh of relief. Opening the rest of the windows, we grabbed a couple of magazines off a shelf and started fanning the air. A few minutes later, the smell of gas was gone.

"Is it okay to come in now?"

Vee stood in the doorway with Jillian right behind her. We waved them inside and showed them the newest message.

"Do me a favor," Vee said, crumpling the note in her hand. "Don't tell anybody about this. My agent will flip out. He's already trying to stop the whole production."

Jillian sat down on the sofa next to her. "Maybe that isn't such a bad idea, Vee. Someone is trying to kill you. Aren't you scared?"

Vee looked down at the floor. "Yes. But I'm more scared of not having a video ready for the VTV premiere next Friday. They've been advertising it for weeks. My fans will go ballistic if we cancel it."

Jillian put her hand on Vee's shoulder. "Your fans will understand. Believe me, I should know."

Vee looked up and smiled. "Thanks, Jillian. But

I'm going to finish this video . . . if it's the last thing I do."

I didn't like the sound of that.

"Just do me a favor," she said to all of us, flashing that famous smile of hers. "Keep an eye out for me, okay?"

No problem.

The rest of the day's shoot went off without a hitch. Vee managed to talk her agent into letting her film the astronaut scene. And I have to admit she "moonwalked" like a pro.

Afterward, Frank and I went back to the hotel. Aunt Trudy was waiting for us at the poolside café, snacking on chips and salsa and sipping a big pink cocktail served in a hollowed-out pineapple.

"So how did it go today, boys?" she asked.

"Great," I said. Then I described Vee's mermaid and astronaut scenes.

Of course, I didn't tell her about Vee nearly drowning or the leaking gas pipe.

"How was *your* day, Aunt Trudy?"

"Fabulous!" she gushed. "Betty and I had a ball! First we had lunch in one of those trendy restaurants on Rodeo Drive. Then we went on the bus tour of celebrity homes."

"That sounds cool," said Frank. "See some nice cribs, Aunt Trudy?"

"Cribs? You could hardly call them cribs, Frank. These were the biggest mansions I've ever seen! Absolutely beautiful! And you should *see* the place where Vee Sharp lives!"

I raised an eyebrow. "Vee's house is part of the tour?"

"Yes! And what a palace! It's huge . . . and very modern, with a Japanese garden and a big pond and a fancy iron gate. Gorgeous. I wish I could have seen what it looks like inside."

"Me too," I muttered under my breath.

Frank kicked me under the table.

"Do you still have the brochure for the bus tour?" he asked Aunt Trudy. "Maybe Joe and I will check it out after dinner."

"Let me see," she said, reaching for her purse. She worked her way through the pockets and pulled out a piece of paper. "Here it is. And look— you could probably catch the last tour of the day."

Frank studied the tour schedule. "You're right, Aunt Trudy. What do you say, Joe? Want to check out your girlfriend's house?"

"Want to stop teasing me about Vee?"

"No."

Aunt Trudy shushed us and flagged down a waiter. "Let's order now," she said. "Or else Joe will *never* get to see his girlfriend's house."

After dinner Frank and I left the hotel and walked to the tour bus stop. We made it in the nick of time. The bright blue bus pulled up to the curb just as we were crossing the street.

"Hurry up, boys," shouted the tour guide, a short chubby guy with thick glasses. "Climb aboard."

It was a little embarrassing to get on such a cheesy-looking bus. The sides featured a big cartoon sun with a human face. Its eyes were bugging out through a pair of binoculars and its tongue hung down like a panting dog's. In huge letters were the words JOLLY PAULY'S HOLLYWOOD ADVENTURE.

We paid the tour guide, who I assumed was Jolly Pauly, and took a seat in between an older couple who appeared to be asleep and a young family with a pair of crying kids.

"Hello, ladies and germs," said the tour guide, speaking into a microphone. His voice was incredibly nasal and sounded way too loud through the bus's speakers. "I'm Jolly Pauly, and this is Jolly Pauly's Hollywood Adventure."

I glanced at Frank and rolled my eyes.

"Coming up on your left," the guide continued, "is a house that was once owned by the legendary Charlie Chaplin."

"Who?" I said to Frank.

Jolly Pauly heard me. "Who is Charlie Chaplin, you ask? Why, he's the silent screen's original king of comedy. Known as the Little Tramp, he starred in such classic gems as *The Gold Rush*, *City Lights*, and *The Great Dictator*." He stopped and winked at me. "Perhaps you should brush up on your film history, young man."

Frank whispered in my ear, "Perhaps you shouldn't ask any more questions, young man."

I stifled a laugh.

"Now back to the tour, ladies and germs," the jolly guide went on. "On your right is a house that belonged to the beautiful Esther Williams."

I was about to ask "Who?" again but held my tongue.

Forty-five minutes later, all of the mansions started to look alike. The tour guide kept listing off the names of "legendary" stars—like Joan Crawford, Greer Garson, Betty Hutton, and a bunch of others I'd never heard of—and I was starting to get bored. In fact, I began to doze off a little.

Finally he said a name I recognized.

"This modern-style mansion belongs to Miss Vee

Sharp, one of today's hottest young music stars."

I snapped awake.

"Stop the bus!" I shouted, jumping to my feet.

Jolly Pauly looked at me as if I were crazy. "Are you serious, young man?"

Frank stood up next to me. "Yes, sir. Could you let us off? Right here? Please?"

"I'm not supposed to let anyone off," the tour guide explained. "It's against the rules."

"But my brother is feeling dizzy," said Frank, nudging me.

I covered my mouth with my hand and puffed out my cheeks. "I'm going to be sick!"

"Not on my bus!" the guide cried, jumping to his feet. "Driver! Pull over!"

The driver slammed on the brakes, and Frank and I climbed off the bus. The tour guide stuck his head out the window. "Do you want us to wait while he . . . ?"

"Hurls?" said Frank. "No, thanks. He needs fresh air right now. I'll call our aunt to pick us up."

The guide shrugged and nodded. I pretended to bend over in pain until the bus disappeared down the road. Then, finally, I stood up and stretched. My legs were half-asleep, and I had to hop up and down on the sidewalk to wake them up.

"Wow. Check it out," said Frank, gazing over my shoulder.

I turned around.

Wow is right.

Vee's home was incredible. A sleek modern mansion made of gleaming white stone and tinted glass, it was set back a hundred feet from the road and surrounded by a rolling green landscape of exotic plants, rock gardens, and reflecting pools. I walked up to the black iron gate for a better look.

"Well? Can you see your girlfriend?" asked Frank.

"Drop it, dude."

The sun was setting fast. As the sky darkened, I began to make out shapes moving behind the large glass windows of the house.

"Look!" Frank said, pointing. "There she is!"

I squinted my eyes and, sure enough, I recognized Vee's slender silhouette outlined against the sunset. It looked like she was talking to someone. Her arms waved in the air and flopped to her sides. Then her whole posture changed. Her shoulders slumped down—as if she were upset about something.

Suddenly a smaller figure walked up behind her.

Her little sister.

"Look, Frank! It's Kay!"

The younger girl raised her arm and pointed her finger at Vee. It looked like she was yelling and accusing her sister.

"This looks bad, Frank," I said. "I wish we could get closer to the house. I'm worried about Vee being alone with Kay."

"What are we supposed to do, Joe? Climb the fence and break in?"

I glanced up at the iron bars. "We *could*, Frank," I said. "We could climb over this gate and get a closer look . . . no problem."

Frank sighed. "Are you crazy? That's trespassing."

"And if Kay kills Vee, that's murder."

My brother took a deep breath. "Okay, Joe. We'll do it. But let's wait a few minutes until the sun goes down."

It didn't take long before the whole neighborhood was plunged into darkness. A pair of tall rectangular lamps illuminated the front gate—so Frank and I ducked into the shadows of a large bamboo plant.

"Okay," I whispered. "I'll go first."

"Do you need a boost?"

"Dude. I'm not a wimp."

I grabbed a couple of the bars with my hands, pulled myself off the ground, and started shimmying upward. I'd almost reached the top when I felt my legs slipping.

"Um, Frank. About that boost . . ."

"I thought you said . . ."

"Just give me a boost!"

My brother pushed and up I went. Soon I was scrambling over the top. It was an eight-foot jump to the ground on the other side. At least I would land on grass.

I jumped.

"Oof."

Hitting the ground with a soft thud, I tripped, stumbled, and rolled across the grass.

"Real smooth," whispered Frank.

"Let's see if you can do any better."

To my surprise, he did. I didn't even have to give him a boost through the bars. Up and over, he scaled the fence like a professional gymnast. After he landed perfectly on his feet, I couldn't resist rating his jump.

"Nine point two."

"Give me a break. That was a ten."

"Your dismount's a little weak."

"So is your brain."

We stopped talking and headed toward the mansion. Small globe lights lit the path through the garden. Creeping through the shadows, we made our way closer—until we saw Vee standing in the window.

She was looking right at us.

"Duck!"

I grabbed Frank by the shoulder and pulled him down next to me behind a large shrub.

"I don't think she saw us," I whispered.

Frank rolled his eyes and shook his head. "Do you realize what we're doing, Joe? We're stalking a celebrity."

"No, we're *protecting* a celebrity."

My brother never got a chance to respond.

A loud alarm pierced the silence.

Giant floodlights lit up the yard.

The sound of barking grew louder behind us.

10.

Boys Behind Bars

I don't believe this.

That's what I thought as we took off running toward the fence—with three huge Dobermans snapping at our heels.

I'm going to kill my brother.

That's what I thought when the police showed up—and arrested us for breaking and entering.

Joe and I were immediately handcuffed and taken to a Los Angeles police station for further questioning. I asked if we could make a phone call, but the police wanted to photograph and finger-print us first.

We're criminals now.

"You're not going to call Aunt Trudy, are you?" Joe asked before I dialed the phone.

"Are you kidding? She'd have a heart attack. I'm calling Dad."

As a former cop, he would know how to handle the situation.

"Hello?"

Unfortunately, Mom picked up the phone. She and Dad were about to sit down to dinner—and she wanted to know all about Hollywood and the video shoot.

"Everything's great, Mom," I lied. "The video is a lot of hard work, but it's fun. I'll tell you all about it later. Right now, I need to ask Dad a question."

She passed the phone to my father. I wasted no time telling him exactly what had happened. And he didn't mince any words because Mom could hear what he was saying.

"Don't worry. I'll take care of it."

That's all he said. The phone went dead. I looked at Joe and shrugged, then a police officer escorted us back to our cell.

Twenty minutes later a tall, barrel-chested cop with a thick Brooklyn accent unlocked the door.

"I'm Officer Daniels," he told us. "I used to work with your father on the force back in New York. You're free to go."

We followed him past a long row of jail cells and into the main lobby.

"Did you talk to our dad?" I asked the officer.

"Yeah. He told me that you boys were doing a little undercover work for him."

"Is that why you're letting us go?"

Officer Daniels shook his head. "Actually, Ms. Sharp dropped all the charges." He nodded across the room.

Vee Sharp sat on a bench reading a magazine.

"Vee!" Joe blurted out.

The pop star looked up and smiled. "Bad boys, bad boys," she sang sweetly. "You know, I was going to bake you a cake with a file in it, but I decided it was easier this way."

We rushed over, laughing.

"We're really sorry about this, Vee," I said.

"Totally. We were just looking out for you," Joe explained. "Honest."

Vee squinted her eyes. "Why should I trust a pair of ex-convicts?"

"Because you live for danger?" Joe offered.

Vee pointed and winked. "You got that right," she said, standing up. "Come on, boys. I'll give you a lift back to your hotel."

Aunt Trudy almost fell off her bar stool when she saw Joe and me pull up in Vee Sharp's red BMW convertible.

"Now *that's* what I call star treatment," she said, waving from the poolside bar.

"That's our Aunt Trudy," Joe explained to Vee. "Please don't say anything about us getting arrested."

"Your secret's safe with me." She stood up and waved across the pool. "Hi, Aunt Trudy!"

We climbed out, said good night to Vee, and watched her drive off into the night. Then we joined Aunt Trudy at the pool bar.

"So, boys," she said, sipping a soda. "I guess this means that you got to go inside Vee Sharp's house."

No, but we were inside a jailhouse.

"Yes, Aunt Trudy," I lied.

"And?" she asked. "Is it just as beautiful as the outside?"

Joe started to making up stuff to tell her about Vee's house. I decided it was my chance to slip away and call Dad on my cell phone. Circling around to the other side of the pool house, I speed-dialed his private number.

"Hello?"

"Dad, it's Frank."

"Are you out of jail?"

"Yes. Vee Sharp dropped the charges."

"Yes, I know. Officer Daniels told me that she showed up at the station."

"Did you tell him about our mission?"

"Not everything. Of course, he doesn't know that you're official agents for ATAC. But he knows that Vee is in danger. I asked him to do me a favor and send in some cops to check out the set tonight."

"But Dad! Vee doesn't want anyone to know! She's afraid the press will find out."

"Don't worry. No one is going to know. I promise."

The next morning Joe and I had to fight our way through a mob of reporters at the studio entrance.

"Do you boys know Vee Sharp?"

"Do you have any idea who's trying to kill her?"

"Do you think this will help or hurt her career?"

The questions came flying, fast and furious. And the cameras' flashbulbs were blinding our eyes.

"Let them through! Let them through!" shouted the security guard.

I pushed Joe through the crowd.

"Hey, you! Joe Hardy!" one of the reporters yelled. "Are you Vee Sharp's new boyfriend?"

My brother stopped and stared back. "How do you know my name?" he asked.

The reporter changed the subject. "Have you set a wedding date yet?"

Joe's jaw dropped open. "A wedding date?"

The reporter started writing in his notepad. "I guess the answer is yes."

"No!"

"No? So you two have broken up?"

Joe gawked. "Broken up? We haven't even had a single date!"

Another reporter stepped forward. "Are you planning to ask her out, Joe?" she said, pointing a microphone.

Joe started stammering. I gave him a shove and pushed him toward the gate.

Another reporter's voice boomed out above the others.

"WHY DID VEE SHARP BAIL YOU OUT OF JAIL?"

Joe and I froze.

They know!

"WHY WERE YOU TWO STALKING HER?"

Oh, no.

I felt my face turning red, but I didn't want the reporters to see me rattled. I ducked my head down and slipped through the gate, shoving Joe ahead of me. The reporters went crazy, firing off more questions and snapping more photos.

If this is what it's like to be famous, I'd rather be a total nobody.

It was too late now. The press knew who we were. They knew we'd been arrested. And they knew that Vee Sharp had gotten us out of jail.

I could just see tomorrow's headline: POP STAR FREES PRISON PALS!

What if Aunt Trudy reads it?

I was almost tempted to turn around and try to straighten things out with the reporters. But I knew it would be a big mistake. They would just twist my words and make everything worse.

"No more questions!" I shouted.

Joe and I started to head for Building A when a loud siren started blaring. We turned around to see what it was.

An ambulance zoomed around the corner.

"Move back!" yelled the security guard. "Everybody, move back!"

"What's this?" Joe muttered.

Lights flashing and siren screaming, the ambulance whizzed past the mob of reporters and zipped through the studio gates.

It stopped in front of Building A.

"No way," Joe said, gasping.

Two paramedics hopped out of the ambulance. They grabbed a stretcher and dashed into the soundstage.

Joe took off after them.

I tried to catch up, stumbling through the doorway and tripping over cables. Inside, people were
rushing around in a panic, waving the paramedics
toward the back of the building.

"Hurry! Before it's too late!" someone yelled.

Too late?

I charged forward, hurdling over the fake craters
on the moon set. When I reached the rear entrance,
I almost collided with my brother. He stood frozen
in the doorway, staring outward.

"No! It can't be," he said.

I looked over to see the paramedics put the
stretcher down.

They were in front of Vee's trailer.

"Please, be okay, Vee," Joe whispered. "Please, be
okay."

Most of the crew had gathered around the Mansion on Wheels. Everyone was quiet.

"I'm going in," Joe announced.

I grabbed my brother by the shoulders. "No,
Joe. You'll only be in the way. Let the paramedics
do their job."

He clenched his teeth. "I just have to know what's
going on."

Brewster Fink came up behind us.

"Brace yourself, guys," he said.

We turned and looked at him.

"What's going on, Brewster?" Joe asked. "What happened?"

Brewster took a deep breath.

"Vee's been poisoned."

11.
Poison Pen

Poisoned?

I wanted to scream at the top of my lungs.

Why? Why weren't we here to stop it?

My stomach twisted into one giant knot. If Vee was murdered while Frank and I wrangled with those stupid reporters, I wouldn't be able to live with myself.

I stared at Vee's trailer.

What's going on in there?

I saw somebody inside walking past a window.

Vee?

No. It was one of the paramedics. But I couldn't see what she was doing.

"We screwed up, Frank," I whispered. "We were supposed to protect her."

My brother put his hand on my shoulder. "Don't jump to conclusions, Joe. We still don't know what happened. Maybe it's not Vee in there."

I looked him in the eye. "What do you mean?"

"I don't see Jillian here. Maybe she's inside the trailer. Maybe she's . . ."

He stopped talking and sighed.

Suddenly the trailer door swung open—and Jillian Goode popped her head out.

"She's okay, everybody!" she shouted.

The whole crew cheered.

"Oh, thank *goodness*!" Spider Jones wailed. "I thought my video was *finished*!"

I shot the skinny director a dirty look. "Is that all you think about? Your stupid video?" I asked him. "What about Vee?"

Spider shrugged. "You heard what Jillian said. Vee is okay! *Okay?*"

I was about to give that freak a piece of my mind when Jillian started waving at us.

"Joe! Frank! Come here! Vee wants to talk to you!"

I turned away from Spider and followed my brother into the trailer. Jillian ushered us quickly inside.

"Hi, guys!"

Vee smiled up at us from her lounge chair—and she looked as healthy as ever.

"Vee!" I said, rushing over. "Are you all right?"

"She's a very lucky girl," said one of the paramedics. "She started to drink from this."

He held a popular brand of bottled water in his gloved hands.

"Water?" said Frank.

The paramedic pointed to a handwritten message on the label.

It read: NUMBER 4: POISON.

"I saw the handwriting when I tilted the bottle to take a drink," Vee explained. "I spit it out immediately."

The paramedic looked at her. "Are you sure you don't want to come to the emergency room with us, Ms. Sharp? Just to make sure you didn't swallow anything poisonous?"

Vee shook her head. "Believe me, I'm fine. The water barely touched my lips."

"Whatever you say, Ms. Sharp." The paramedics started packing up their things. "We'll take this to the lab and run some tests. I'm sure the police will want to dust the bottle for fingerprints."

Vee's eyes opened wide. "No police! If we tell

them about this, then the whole studio will be crawling with reporters."

I glanced at Frank.

"Should you tell her or should I?" he said.

The paramedics dropped their heads, grabbed their bags, and left the trailer quickly.

Vee looked up at us. "What?"

I cleared my throat. "The reporters are already waiting at the front gate. They assaulted Frank and me with questions. They know you got us out of jail last night."

Vee groaned and flopped back in her chair. "What next?"

"Maybe you should just call it a day, Vee," I suggested. "Go home and get some rest."

"Are you kidding? The reporters will be waiting for me there, too." She stood up and started pacing her trailer. "I'll tell you what I'm going to do. I'm going to stay right here and finish this video! Jillian, go tell Spider that I'm getting ready for the next scene."

She walked to her vanity table and started applying makeup. I guess she liked to do it herself.

"Are you sure you want to do this, Vee?" Frank asked.

She nodded. "Today's our last day in the studio.

Then we have a location shoot tomorrow, and the video's done. I can't stop now. People are depending on me."

I walked up behind her, catching her eye in the mirror. "Okay, Vee. You're the star."

"And don't you forget it," she said teasingly. "Now get back to work, you two. I'm sure Brewster has something for you to do."

She was right. As soon as Frank and I walked onto the soundstage, the bearded production manager grabbed us by the shoulders and pointed us toward the front entrance.

"See that four-wheeler cart by the door?" he asked. We nodded, and Brewster continued. "I want you two to wheel it over to the main gate. There's a big shipment waiting for us there. Load up the sacks and bring them to the front of the building. Got it?"

We got it.

The cart was pretty big but easy to push. It took just a couple of minutes to steer it through the lot to the main gate.

That was the easy part.

The hard part was watching Vee's agent, Jackson Puck, talk to all the reporters outside the gate.

"It looks like he's giving an interview," said Frank.

"Yeah," I agreed. "A big interview."

There were dozens of microphones and TV news cameras pointed right at Jackson.

That's weird. Vee wanted to keep everything hush-hush.

We parked the cart next to the security booth and moved closer to hear what he was saying.

"Vee Sharp is one of the world's greatest pop sensations. A star like her will always have a few crazy fans," he told the reporters. "Sometimes these fans can be quite dangerous."

He held up several pieces of paper and showed them to the crowd.

I can't believe he's doing this.

They were the death threats Vee had received— the Top Ten Ways to Die.

"Look!" I said to Frank. "He's showing them the messages! Vee would flip out if she knew he was talking to the press!"

Jackson Puck adjusted his toupee and continued talking.

"These are just a few of the notes Ms. Sharp has received in recent weeks," he announced to the mob. "In addition to these disturbing threats, there have also been several attempts on Vee's life."

The reporters went wild.

"How did the fan try to kill her?"

"Is she scared?"

"Will she finish her new video?"

And the final kicker:

"Are the Hardy boys on the suspect list?"

I couldn't take it any longer.

Shoving through the crowd, I grabbed Jackson Puck by the arm. "What are you doing?" I asked him. "Vee wants to keep all of this quiet!"

Puck shot me a nasty look and sneered. "Look, kid. You're just an intern. I'm her agent, and I know what I'm doing."

"But it's not what Vee wants you to do."

The slimy agent glared at me. "Listen," he muttered under his breath. "This is the story of the year. All of the celebrity news shows are here. *Hollywood Excess. Entertainment Now. Behind the Pop Songs.* You just can't buy publicity like this!"

He pushed me aside and grinned at the reporters.

Then a big gust of wind blew the toupee off his head.

Everybody burst out laughing—and the cameras caught the look of horror on Jackson Puck's face. I walked away and found my brother.

"What happened?" Frank asked. "What did he say to you?"

I looked him in the eye. "He just gave me a very good reason why he might be the one behind all the death threats."

SUSPECT PROFILE

Name: Jackson Puck

Hometown: Los Angeles, CA

Physical description: 42 years old, 6'2", 215 lbs., pot belly, greasy black mustache and toupee, shiny colored suits.

Occupation: Talent agent

Background: Born and raised in Beverly Hills, son of two B-list actors, swore he'd bring fame and honor to the family name, lied his way into a job with a Hollywood talent agency, manipulated his way into owning his own agency.

Suspicious behavior: Seemed delighted with the media attention caused by Vee Sharp's death threats, bragged about the free publicity.

Suspected of: Terrorizing the pop star as a publicity stunt.

Possible motives: Fame, success, record sales, and a big piece of Vee's profits.

Frank and I decided to ignore the rest of Jackson's interview. Instead we asked the security guard about the shipment that Brewster had sent us to pick up.

"Right over there," the guard said, pointing across the lot. "That pile of burlap sacks."

We thanked him and pushed the four-wheeler cart toward the tall mountain of sacks.

"I guess Brewster thinks we're pretty strong," said Frank. "That pile must weigh a ton."

I reached up and lifted one of the overstuffed sacks. "Actually, it's not too heavy," I said.

Frank looked like he didn't believe me. "Yeah, right. Light as a feather, I'm sure."

He grabbed a sack and hefted it onto his shoulder. "You weren't kidding, Joe."

"Hey, bro," I said. "Would I kid you?"

"Would an agent sell his soul for a big story on *Hollywood Excess*?"

I laughed and helped him load up the cart. A little while later, we were pushing the burlap-covered cargo to Building A. I walked to the doorway and poked my head inside.

"Hey, Brewster! Where do you want this ship-ment?"

Brewster Fink strolled up to us, smiling. "That's

quite a load there. Hope you boys didn't hurt yourselves."

"No," said Frank. "The sacks are pretty light. What's in them?"

"Sawdust."

"Sawdust? What for?"

"For the circus scene."

"Circus scene?"

My mind started racing.

What dangerous thing are they going to make Vee do now? Walk a tightrope? Swing on a trapeze? Stand up on a galloping horse?

"What do you want us to do with all this sawdust?" Frank asked.

"Take it inside," Brewster told us, "and spread it around inside the cage."

Oh, no.

"The cage?" I asked.

"Yeah. The lion's cage."

I can't believe my ears.

"A lion's cage, Brewster?" I said. "You mean, Vee is going to perform with real *live* lions?"

My question was immediately answered—with a loud roar inside the building.

12.

Into the Lion's Den

Lions. Great.

"This is crazy," I said to Joe as we pushed the sacks of sawdust to the back of the building. "Vee is getting death threats every day. Someone has tried to poison her, electrocute her, drown her . . . you name it. And now she's going to do a scene with wild animals?"

Another loud roar made us jump.

Joe and I turned around—and there they were. Two massive beasts with long manes and sharp claws, the lions paced back and forth inside a small cage on wheels.

One of them spotted us and growled.

"Pretty scary," Joe had to admit.

Brewster Fink walked over to us. "Hey, boys.

Start spreading the sawdust inside the circus cage. Then the animal trainer can unload the lions."

We looked at the large round cage in the center of the soundstage. Behind it the crew was hanging backdrops painted with cartoon clowns and wagons and elephants. I glanced at Joe.

"Vee isn't going inside the cage with the lions, is she?" he asked.

Brewster laughed. "Of course she is!"

Joe and I were speechless.

Brewster laughed again and pointed to a machine with a lever, a wheel, and a steel cable. "Watch this," he said, pulling the lever.

The wheel started turning and unrolling the cable. Above the round cage, a large panel of iron bars began to lower down. It divided the cage perfectly in half.

"You see?" said Brewster. "Vee will be in one half, and the lions will be in the other half. The camera will be placed over here, right in the middle, so the divider will be blocked from view. It'll just *look* like they're in the cage together."

Joe and I weren't convinced.

Something can go wrong.

But Brewster was in no mood to argue with us. "Now get to work on that sawdust."

He raised the divider, and Joe and I started

hauling the sacks into the cage. Dumping them out one by one, we spread the sawdust evenly across the floor.

The lions roared at us the whole time.

"I don't like this, Frank," said my brother. "Do you see the claws on those man-eaters? They could reach right through the bars and . . ."

He stopped talking. I could see how worried he was. I knew that he liked Vee a lot—even if they hadn't set a wedding date.

When we finished the job, the animal trainer wheeled the lions over to the cage and unleashed them. The two giant beasts leaped out and roared, kicking up sawdust with every stroke of their paws. The trainer stepped into the cage with them. Cracking a whip, he tried to force them toward the far end of the cage.

The lions weren't thrilled about it.

In fact, they fought the trainer every step of the way. They opened their jaws and roared—exposing long rows of razor-sharp teeth.

The trainer cracked the whip. The lions backed off.

"Okay! Lower the divider!" he shouted.

Brewster pushed the lever, and the steel bars came down, trapping the lions in the far end of the cage.

"See, boys?" said Brewster. "It's one hundred percent safe."

I looked at Joe. He winced.

"Let's go talk to Vee," he said. "I don't think she should do this."

I followed him out to the trailer. As he reached up to knock, the door swung open. Out stepped Vee.

She was dressed as a ringmaster.

"Hi, guys," she greeted us. "What do you think of my outfit? Pretty cool, huh?"

She spun around and showed off her white puffy pants, tall black boots, and red fitted jacket. Her hair was swept up and tucked inside a tall black hat.

"Stand back, boys."

She cracked a whip in the air.

Joe and I tried to laugh—but we were too worried to enjoy the fashion show.

"What's wrong?" she asked, seeing our faces.

Joe took a step forward. "We don't think you should do the scene, Vee. It's too dangerous."

Vee frowned. "Look," she said. "I've been practicing with the animal trainer. And I'll be separated from the lions. It's totally safe."

"Like the goldfish bowl?" I pointed out. "And the tarantulas?"

"Yeah, Vee," said Joe. "On this set, even the bottled water is dangerous."

Vee sighed and leaned back against the trailer. "Maybe you're right," she said. "Maybe I shouldn't do the lion-taming scene."

"WHAT?"

Spider Jones came bustling toward us, his spiky hair standing on end.

"You *must* do the lion-taming scene, Vee!" he cried. "My artistic vision *depends* on it!"

I was starting to get *real* tired of this guy. Sure, he was a hot-shot music video director. But he didn't care about Vee—or her safety—at all.

"I don't understand, Mr. Jones," I said politely. "What kind of artistic vision is worth risking Vee's life?"

Spider turned and glared at me. At first it looked like he was going to blow up at me. Then he took a deep breath and explained himself.

"I see Vee Sharp as a role model for young girls. I see her as a strong and powerful leader. I see her as a black widow who rules her web. I see her as a mermaid who hypnotizes with her beauty. I see her as the first woman on the moon. I see her as a lion tamer and a superhero . . . and so much more."

I looked the director in the eye. "Do you want to see her dead, too?"

Spider grunted. "Of course not."

"Look, Mr. Jones," said Joe, stepping forward.

"We're not asking you to cancel the shoot or anything. We want you to come up with a safer way to film Vee with the lions."

"Yeah," I said. "What if you put her *outside* the cage and used special effects to add more bars in the editing room?"

Spider shook his head. "It's too expensive. And it's too late now anyway. Everything is set and ready to go. Do you know how much time and money we'd lose if we changed it now?"

We stood there in silence.

Brewster Fink walked out of the building and approached us. "We're all set, Spider." He looked at Vee and grinned. "Are you ready to tame some lions?"

Everyone looked at Vee.

She took a deep breath and stared thoughtfully at the ground. Then she lifted her head and flashed her world-famous smile.

"I'm ready."

The lions had finally calmed down.

"Places, everyone! Places!"

The director sat down in his chair, and the crew backed away from the cage. I joined Joe and Jillian next to the cable machine that lifted and lowered the divider.

I wanted to keep my eye on that lever.

"Keep your fingers crossed," I whispered to Jillian.

"Don't worry," she said. "Vee isn't afraid of the lions. I watched the trainer give her lessons last week. She's cool about all this."

Jillian was trying to act brave. But I could tell she was nervous by the way she dug her fingers into her notebook. She held it so tightly to her chest, I was afraid she was going to rip the binding in half.

"What's in the notebook?" I asked.

"Oh, this? I'm keeping track of things for Vee. I'm hoping she'll hire me as her personal assistant."

I nodded and turned my attention to Spider Jones, who was giving last-minute directions to his star.

"Okay, Vee. Before we film you with the lions, I want to get some shots of you singing the lyrics. When the music starts, walk slowly along the cage right here and sing directly to the camera. It's on a track so it can follow along as you move."

Vee nodded.

"Okay! Places!" Spider yelled.

Vee took her spot inside the cage, glancing at the lions on the other side of the divider. She tried to hide her nervousness with a smile. Then the camera rolled up along the outside of the cage, the lens pointing at the bars.

"Ready? *Camera!* And *music!*"

There was a short pause. At first all you could hear was the soft whir of the camera. Then, suddenly, the sound of loud music blasted across the stage.

Vee's hit song, "Girls Rule," exploded from a pair of speakers.

The lions leaped.

And roared.

Loudly.

Vee Sharp jumped back—and missed her cue.

"Cut! Cut! CUT!" yelled the director. "Turn off the music!"

The song was stopped—but the lions kept roaring.

"I'm sorry, Spider," said Vee. "The lions startled me."

The animal trainer approached them. "Sorry, Ms. Sharp, but the lions don't seem to like your music very much," he explained.

Vee shrugged. "Everyone's a critic, it seems."

"Could we shoot the scene in silence?" asked the trainer.

Spider frowned. "No. We need to play the music so Vee can lip-synch. The lions will just have to deal with it."

"Well, maybe you could lower the volume," the trainer suggested.

Spider agreed.

The soundman adjusted the levels, and everybody took their places again.

"CAMERA! And MUSIC!"

Vee's song flowed through the speakers—at a much lower volume.

But the lions still hated it.

They growled and roared. They clawed at the air. They ran circles inside the cage.

Vee shuddered—and missed her cue again.

But that wasn't going to stop Spider Jones. "Vee! Just *ignore* the lions! Cameraman! Keep rolling! Soundman! Start the song again! From the top!"

The music screeched to a halt. Vee tried to collect herself, but it wasn't easy. The lions kept roaring at her through the divider.

I glanced at Joe.

Man, he's even more nervous than Jillian.

Both of them stared anxiously toward the cage. In fact, the entire video crew seemed to be holding their breath.

The music started again.

The lions snarled—but Vee took her director's advice and ignored them. With a flirty smile, she started singing along with the recording.

"Girls . . . girls . . . girls rule. . . ."

Spider grinned and waved his star forward. Vee

began walking along the bars of the cage, the camera tracking her every move.

"Look out, boys," she crooned. "Girls rule. . . ."

I was definitely impressed. Vee seemed to be in full control, singing the song and strutting her stuff with loads of attitude. She didn't look scared at all.

That's when everything went wrong.

The closer Vee got to the divider, the wilder the lions seemed to get.

Suddenly one of them swiped at her through the bars.

Vee screamed.

Staggering backward, she stumbled to the ground. The crew jumped up in a panic, and the director started yelling.

I grabbed Joe by the arm—to keep him from rushing into the scene.

But we should have been watching Jillian Goode.

The young fan was swooning beside us. The blood suddenly rushed from her face. Her eyes flickered. Then she fainted and collapsed.

On top of the lever!

Joe and I lunged to catch her.

But it was too late.

The steel divider started rising up in the cage. Vee Sharp was trapped inside. . . .

With two very angry lions.

13.

Claws of Death

The lions rushed forward.

"Vee!" I gasped.

The whole crew froze in place—and watched in helpless horror as the savage beasts circled around the pop star.

Vee stood in the center of the cage, gripping the whip in both hands. She turned her head from one lion to the other, not sure what to do.

They growled—and moved in closer.

Suddenly somebody pushed past a group of stagehands and rushed to the door of the cage.

It was the animal trainer.

Yes! Help her!

The stocky man flung open the door and

stepped inside. "SIT! DOWN!" he shouted, cracking his whip.

The lions turned their heads. First they simply stared at the guy. Then they attacked.

"Look out!" Vee shrieked.

But it was too late.

One of the lions lashed out with its claws, knocking the whip from the trainer's hand. The other one pounced, shoving him backward—and out of the cage.

Down he went.

Bang!

The trainer's head smashed against the base of a spotlight. The blow knocked him out cold.

Clang!

A stagehand slammed the cage door shut before the lion could escape. The beast bounced against the bars and fell into the sawdust.

But that only seemed to make him angrier.

Scrambling to its feet, the lion joined its partner in the center of the cage, where Vee stood as helpless as a baby lamb. The lions' eyes glistened as they licked their chops with long pink tongues.

One of them took a step toward her, growling.

Vee raised the whip—and brought it down hard with a quick clean jerk.

Crack!

Sawdust flew into the air, showering down over the lion's face. The beast grunted and backed off.

That's when the other one went after her.

"Vee! Look out!" I yelled.

Her head snapped around, her eyes zeroing in on the other feline predator. It hunched down on it back legs—and prepared to pounce.

Crack!

Vee's whip whizzed through the air, spraying the lion with sawdust.

Go get 'em, Vee!

In my heart I was cheering. But in my brain, I knew Vee wouldn't be able to keep both of the lions at bay for very long. Sooner or later, the so-called king of the jungle would win the fight.

And Vee would get hurt—or worse.

I have to do something. Now.

Opening my mouth as wide as I could, I unleashed a loud battle cry from the depths of my throat. Then I charged straight at the cage. The lions turned their heads, curious and confused. I had no idea what I was going to do once I reached the cage—but I would think of something.

"Joe! No!" Vee screamed.

My body slammed against the cage with a thud. Poking my arms through the bars, I teased and coaxed the baffled beasts by fluttering my fingers at them.

"Here, kitty, kitty, kitty," I cooed.

One of the lions seemed to grab the bait. He turned and walked toward me while the other gazed on silently.

"What's new, pussycat?"

My hand dipped back and forth a few feet from its face. The lion followed my fingers with its eyes—and licked its teeth.

Down, down, down, I lowered my hand all the way to the ground. Then I grabbed a big handful of the sawdust—and threw it in the lion's face.

"ARRRRAAUGH!"

The animal went crazy. Yelping, twitching, and rolling onto its back, the lion pawed its face furiously to shake off the sawdust.

I looked up at Vee. A huge smile spread over her face. But then her attention turned to the other lion.

It was circling around her, moving faster and closer with every step.

"Hey! Cat! Want a piece of me?"

Who said that?

My gaze shifted to the other side of the cage. I quickly spotted a pair of hands poking through the bars.

It was Frank.

Nice!

"Come and get it, *fat cat*!" he taunted the beast.

The lion turned around—and charged after Frank.

Whoosh!

My brother threw a big handful of sawdust in the animal's furry face.

"ARRRRRAUGHHH!"

The beast went down with a roar, shaking its head from side to side. I started to relax—when the other lion came after me.

"Joe!" Vee screamed.

I ducked down to grab more sawdust.

But I didn't move fast enough.

The lion's claw slashed across my face. With a powerful jerk, I went flying backward, knocked senseless by the force of the lion's huge paw.

"Joe!" Vee shrieked.

She started to run toward me. My brother shouted at her, "Vee! Stop! Head for the door!"

In a daze, I glanced up to see her bolting for the door of the cage while Frank threw another handful of sawdust at the angry lions. One of the stagehands flung open the door. Vee dashed through and . . .

SLAM!

The door swung shut.

Vee was free.

I closed my eyes and flopped backward onto the floor. A stream of blood trickled across my face.

Ouch!

The next thing I knew, Vee was leaning down over me, holding my head in her arms.

"Joe? Are you all right? Can you hear me, Joe?"

I gazed into her eyes. "Hey," I said softly. "Aren't you that famous singer? Can I have your autograph?"

She laughed and hugged me. "Thanks, Joe," she whispered. "You saved my life."

She helped me to my feet. I felt a little stunned, but all in all, I was okay.

"You're bleeding." Vee pointed to my left cheek. "Maybe you should see a doctor. You might need stitches."

I reached up and touched the wound. "It's just a scratch," I assured her. "Where's Frank? I'm not the only hero around here."

"He's helping Jillian."

I turned around and saw my brother helping Jillian to her feet. She looked incredibly pale and a little shaky. Frank had to slip his arm around her to keep her standing. Vee and I walked over to help them out.

"I'm *so* sorry, Vee," Jillian whimpered. "It was all

my fault. I fainted and hit the lever and I'm sorry. Can you forgive me?"

Vee smiled. "Next time, watch where you're standing! But of course, Jillian—I know this was an accident. You should come to my trailer and lie down. You're as white as a ghost."

Jillian nodded weakly. Frank handed her off to Vee, who helped the girl back to the trailer.

I looked at Frank. "Thanks, bro," I told him. "I couldn't have done it alone."

He shrugged and said, "I know." Then he added, "You're bleeding."

"I know."

We laughed. Brewster Fink walked toward us with a first-aid kit. "Okay, Mr. Hero," he said. "You saved the day . . . again. But I'm not letting you do any more work until I fix up that scratch on your face. It's the least I can do."

The big bearded guy cleaned the wound and applied a large bandage. Meanwhile Frank paced back and forth, staring at the floor. Then he turned his back to us and picked up a notebook.

"You're good as new," said Brewster, slapping my back. "Good job, man."

"Thanks, dude."

As soon as Brewster walked away, Frank turned

SUSPECT PROFILE

__Name:__ Jillian Goode

__Hometown:__ San Diego, CA

__Physical description:__ 16 years old, 5'7", 120 lbs., pretty, strawberry blond hair.

__Occupation:__ High school student, president of the Vee Sharp Fan Club

__Background:__ Daughter of a former model, she grew up wishing to be part of the Hollywood scene; always felt unattractive and overweight; longs to be liked and accepted by "the beautiful people."

__Suspicious behavior:__ Devoted her life to pop star Vee Sharp, attended every concert and talked her way onto the set of Vee's music video, fainted and hit the lever that unleashed the lions, wrote strange things about Vee in her notebook.

__Suspected of:__ Stalking, threatening, and attempting to kill Vee Sharp.

__Possible motives:__ Jealousy, obsession, insanity.

around and held up the notebook. "You have to see this, Joe."

"What is it?"

"Jillian's notebook."

He handed it to me. I opened it and started flipping through—and I was totally shocked by what I saw.

Most of the pages were filled with Vee Sharp's name, written over and over again in different styles. Sometimes the letters were curly or loopy. Other times they were blocky and bold.

Vee Sharp. *Vee Sharp*. VEE SHARP.

Again and again, page after page.

"This is really weird," I muttered.

"Yes, it is. But wait till you see *this*." He reached over and flipped to the end. He pointed to the page. I looked down and gasped.

It said: VEE'S LAST DAY: CUT & DIE.

I looked up at my brother. "What does this mean?" I asked him.

He stared down grimly. "It means that Jillian Goode is one of our prime suspects."

I looked at Frank and shook my head.

"It's hard to believe that Jillian would do this," I said. "She loves Vee."

"Maybe a little too much."

"Oh, come on, Frank. Do you really think Jillian is capable of hurting someone? She's one of the sweetest girls I've ever met. And one of the coolest girls you ever had a crush on."

Frank lowered his head and blushed. "Yes, but . . . what about this notebook?"

I glanced down and stared at the words again.

CUT & DIE.

"Maybe we should just ask her about it," I suggested.

Frank looked up at me. "Maybe you're right."

I threw my arm over his shoulder and steered my brother toward the trailer out back. In my mind, I *knew* there must be a logical explanation for the crazy stuff in Jillian's notebook. She wasn't a cold-blooded killer. I was sure of it.

But then I heard a loud piercing sound coming from inside the trailer.

Vee was screaming.

14.
Cut!

"Jillian! Stop!"

Vee screamed again, even louder. Joe and I dashed to the trailer. Without bothering to knock, we flung open the door and scrambled inside.

I'm not sure what we expected to see: Jillian strangling Vee? Jillian attacking Vee with a weapon?

What we *didn't* expect to see was the two girls reading a newspaper—and laughing hysterically.

"Vee! Are you okay?" said Joe.

The girls looked up and stopped laughing. Jillian quickly stashed the newspaper behind her back. Vee had a guilty look on her face.

"What's going on?" I asked. "We heard screaming."

"Oh, it's nothing," Jillian answered. "We were just laughing over something. Girl stuff."

I glanced down at the newspaper.

Vee sighed. "You might as well show it to them, Jillian. They're going to see it sooner or later."

Jillian handed me the newspaper. It was one of those cheesy gossip papers you see at the checkout line of grocery stores—the kind that features the latest celebrity scandal.

But this time, Joe and I were on the front cover.

"Give me a break," my brother muttered.

The headline read: VEE SHARP'S SECRET SHOCKER: BROTHERS BATTLE FOR HER HEART—AND LAND IN JAIL!

There was a photo of Joe and me walking out of the police station. The picture was ripped in half so that we were separated by a huge color shot of Vee. Her lips were puckered up—like she was ready to kiss one of us.

Joe's eyes bugged out as he started to read the story. "This is ridiculous! It's nothing but lies!"

Vee shrugged. "Welcome to Hollywood, boys."

We gathered around the paper and giggled over the phony story. The reporter claimed that Joe and I got into a fistfight at Vee's house—and the star couldn't decide which one of us she liked more.

No wonder the girls were screaming with laughter.

I was laughing too. But then I remembered that Jillian was still a suspect. In fact, I was holding the evidence in my hands.

Jillian's notebook.

I waited until the girls finished reading the story. Then I cleared my throat and held up the notebook. "Jillian, you dropped this."

She stared at it and blinked her eyes. "Oh! Thanks!"

"I hope you don't mind, but I flipped through to find out who it belonged to," Joe said. It was a lie— but we definitely needed it. "Hey, why did you write Vee's name in it so many times?"

Jillian didn't hesitate with her answer. "Oh, that. Vee wanted me to come up with a new logo for her name. When I told her that I'm studying to become a designer, she asked me to help her out."

Vee nodded. "Yeah, I need a new design for my album covers, T-shirts . . . stuff like that."

That makes sense.

I felt a little guilty bringing it up, but I had to. "What about this?" I asked, opening the notebook to the last page.

Jillian leaned forward and read it out loud. "Vee's last day: cut and die."

She glanced over at Vee—and both of them burst out laughing.

"They think I'm a suspect, Vee!" Jillian said, giggling.

"You can't blame them," Vee told her. "It sounds like a death threat."

Jillian saw the confusion on my face. She stopped laughing and explained. "Vee asked me to remind her to have her hair cut and dyed for the last day of the video shoot."

"My hairstylist hates it when I miss appointments," added Vee.

I started to laugh. "Oh. Well, in that case, the word is D-Y-E, not D-I-E."

Jillian shrugged. "Okay, so I'm not a good speller."

A few minutes later we were called back onto the set. Spider wanted to finish the lion-taming scene—*without* the lions.

"We have enough animal footage," he explained to the crew. "But we need more shots of Vee in her lion-tamer costume. We can put it all together in the editing room."

The lions were quickly wheeled away, and we shot the rest of Vee's scene without a hitch. It was cool to watch her dance and sing with the music. It was even cooler that nobody tried to kill her while she did it.

"CUT! That's a wrap!" Spider announced at the end of the afternoon. "Thank you, everyone! It's been a tough shoot, but *you did it*!"

The crew cheered.

Brewster clapped his hands to get their attention. "Okay, everyone! We're finished here, so please stack up all the props against the far wall! Just one last location shoot tomorrow morning, and the video is in the can. I'll see you all bright and early at the Hollywood sign!"

The crew scattered. Spider folded up his director's chair and took off. Vee was heading back to her trailer, but T-Mix grabbed her on the way.

"Hey! Vee!" he said, jogging up next to her. His long braids bounced as he ran. "I set up a recording studio in the next building. If you've got the time, I'd love for you to do some new vocals for the dance remix of 'Girls Rule.'"

Vee sighed. "Aw, gee, T-Mix. I'm pretty beat. It's been a long day."

"Please, *please*," the record producer begged. "The record company wants to release it as soon as possible. The CD version is still climbing up the charts."

Vee thought about it. "Well, I'm not anxious to

face those reporters. Are they still waiting for me at the front gate?"

"Yup," he said. "At least a dozen of them. I had to push and shove to get past them."

Vee rolled her eyes. "Okay," she agreed. "I might as well stay here and get some work done. Maybe they'll get tired and leave."

She turned to face Joe and me.

"Do you guys want to come and watch me in the recording studio?"

"That would be awesome," said Joe.

"But first we should help move the props," I reminded him. "We could catch up with you later, Vee."

"Great," she said.

"We'll be in Building B," said T-Mix.

The two turned around and walked off. Joe and I joined the crew on the soundstage. I had just started sweeping up when I found a crumpled piece of paper lying in the sawdust.

"Joe, come look at this." I showed him the paper.

It was another death threat: NUMBER 3: WILD ANIMALS.

Joe glanced around the soundstage. "Anybody could have put it there," he said.

I sighed and shoved the note into my pocket. Then we went back to work. It took us almost an hour to tear down the set and stack up all the props.

"Hey, Frank! Help me lift this crater onto the pile!"

Joe stood on his toes, struggling to hoist the plaster prop over his head.

"I don't know, bro," I said. "That pile is pretty high. If you ask me, it looks dangerous."

"Who asked you? Just help me."

I reached up and pushed the fake crater onto the stack. Then I tested the pile with my hand— just to make sure it was stable. I would feel awful if the whole thing came crashing down on top of somebody.

"Does it pass regulation, Mr. Safety?" asked Joe.

"I don't know," I said. "Maybe we shouldn't have stacked it so high."

Joe rolled his eyes. "Come on. It's fine. Let's go to the recording studio. I want hear Vee sing."

We left the soundstage and walked to the building next door. Inside we passed a row of doors until we reached a red sign that said, RECORDING IN SESSION. We peeked in.

T-Mix sat in front of a giant mixing board, fiddling with a bunch of knobs. He glanced up, saw us, and waved us inside.

"Hi, guys," he said. "We're almost done here. Have a seat."

Joe and I sat down in a pair of office chairs and looked through the big glass window above the mixing board. Vee stood in front of a microphone. She had a bulky set of earphones over her head and a tired smile on her face.

"How should I sing the last line, T-Mix?"

"Try shouting it as loud as you can," he said into a small mike. "It should sound gritty and tough."

Vee nodded and looked down. T-Mix pressed a button and the music started. I recognized the final chorus of "Girls Rule,"—except now it was faster and harder, with a loud throbbing dance beat.

"Girls rule! GIRLS RULE!!!" Vee belted out.

"Again," said T-Mix, rewinding the tape.

"GIRLS RULE! GIRLS RULE!"

T-Mix started clapping. "That's it! Perfect! You got it, girl!"

Vee laughed. "So we're done?"

"We're done."

She pulled the earphones off her head and rushed into the mixing room. "Was that tough enough?"

"Listen." T-Mix rewound the tape and played it for her. "Pretty tough, huh?"

Vee smiled and nodded. "I can't wait to hear the final mix," she said.

T-Mix leaned forward and pushed a few buttons. "I'll work on it tonight," he said. "But this will give you an idea of what it will sound like."

He played a selection for us. It was a dance version of "Girls Rule," but it wasn't Vee's voice.

"Wow, that's amazing," said Joe.

"Who is that singing?" I asked.

T-Mix lowered his head and blushed a little. "It's me."

"Man! You're awesome!" said Joe.

"Isn't he?" said Vee.

"Totally," I agreed. "Why are you producing records for other people, T-Mix? You should be singing them yourself."

T-Mix shook his head. "No, man, I belong behind the scenes. Let's face it. I'm just a skinny little guy with big braids and pimples. I don't have 'The Look' that the studios are going for these days."

Vee patted him on the shoulders. "Don't worry, T. Everyone in the record business knows that *you're* the one with the talent. I just show up, and you make the magic happen."

He looked down at the floor. "Thanks, Vee."

We said good night to T-Mix and walked Vee back to her trailer. It was getting dark and the soundstage was empty. It looked like everyone had gone home.

"Come inside for a minute," said Vee, opening the door. "I just have to call my agent and confirm my hair appointment."

Joe and I joined her inside the luxury trailer. While Vee made the calls on her cell phone, my brother and I kicked back and played a video game. I was about to blow up Joe's spaceship when Vee announced that she had left her makeup bag on the soundstage.

"I'll be right back!"

Joe looked up from the game. "Wait! I'll go with you!" He jumped up from his chair—and I destroyed his spaceship on the video screen.

They left me in the trailer. I had pushed the reset button and started to play a solo game when I heard something outside.

A bloodcurdling scream.

It's Vee.

I leaped to my feet, dashed out of the trailer, and charged across the soundstage. Joe and Vee stood against the far wall in front of all the props.

The huge stack had fallen . . .

. . . *on top of somebody.*

A pair of legs stuck out beneath a cluttered pile of steel bars, wooden panels, and plaster props. All we could see were a large pair of men's work boots.

"Hurry!" I said. "Let's move this stuff!"

Joe, Vee, and I started clearing away the wreckage piece by piece. Whoever was buried beneath it all wasn't moving.

The final piece was a heavy wooden crate. Joe had to help me lift it off the body.

Vee gasped.

"No!"

She spun around and started sobbing. Joe and I looked down to see for ourselves.

"I don't believe it," Joe whispered.

Brewster Fink was dead.

JOE

15.
A Very Bad Sign

The police responded quickly. While Frank answered their questions, I took Vee back to her trailer. She was really shaken up by Brewster's death.

"He was more than a crew manager. He was my friend," she cried. "We've been working together for years. He's like a part of my family."

I put my arm around her shoulder.

"Why? Why would anyone want to hurt such a sweet guy?" she asked, weeping gently. "It doesn't make any sense."

I patted her back, not sure what to tell her. Her friend was dead, and nothing I could say would change that. I pulled her into my arms and hugged her.

There was a knock at the door. "It's me. Frank."

"Come in."

He opened the door and stepped into the trailer. "How are you doing, Vee?" he said softly.

She looked up, her eyes puffy and red. "Not so good," she whispered. "What's happening out there? Did the police find anything?"

Frank sat down. "They think there was a struggle. There were scratches on Brewster's face, and they suspect someone pushed the stack of props on top of him."

Vee looked down and shook her head.

Frank continued. "There's something else. The police found a harness underneath Brewster's body. It looked like someone had cut halfway through the straps to weaken it."

"A harness?" I asked.

"Yes. It was the body harness that Vee's supposed to wear during the shoot tomorrow."

"What are you saying?" said Vee. "Brewster sabotaged the strap so I would fall? I don't believe it."

Frank shook his head. "No. I think Brewster walked in and caught the culprit in the act. He was killed because he was a witness."

Vee sighed. "So it's all my fault. Brewster died because some lunatic wants to kill me."

She started to cry again. I hugged her and patted her shoulder. "You should take some time off, Vee,"

I whispered in her ear. "Forget about the video."

She looked up at me. "I'm going to finish this, Joe. Brewster would want me to. As they say in Hollywood, the show must go on."

Frank looked uneasy. "I wouldn't go hanging from a body harness if I were you," he said.

Vee gritted her teeth. "I'm going to do it. Now that we know exactly what the killer is planning, we can double-check the harness and the wires."

"Do me a favor," I said. "Triple-check them."

The next day Aunt Trudy brought us breakfast in bed—along with a copy of the morning paper. "Explain this to me, please," she said.

I rubbed my eyes and looked down at the front page.

The headline read: AMERICA'S DEADLIEST MUSIC VIDEO: VEE SHARP'S CREW MANAGER DEAD ON ARRIVAL.

Frank and I looked up at our aunt. She was incredibly upset. "It says here that there's a killer on the loose," she said. "Someone is stalking Vee Sharp on the set of her video."

I shook my head. "You know how the reporters exaggerate everything, Aunt Trudy. Yesterday they said Frank and I went to jail for fighting over Vee."

Aunt Trudy pursed her lips together. "Did somebody really die yesterday?"

"Yes, but it was just an accident," Frank lied.

"That's awful. Why didn't you tell me?"

"We didn't want you to worry."

Aunt Trudy sat down on the edge of the bed. "Well, you're right. I *am* worried. Maybe you two should skip the last day of shooting."

My jaw dropped. "But Aunt Trudy . . ."

"Those movie sets can be dangerous. My friend Betty has worked on them. She says people get hurt all the time."

Frank sat up in bed. "But it's the last day, Aunt Trudy. Please let us finish our internship. It might help us get into college."

"And we'll be extra careful," I added.

Aunt Trudy weakened. "Oh, all right. But you boys had better stay out of trouble. And don't do anything stupid or dangerous."

"We promise," I said, crossing my fingers beneath the sheets.

After a quick breakfast, Frank and I hopped into the rental car and headed for the Hollywood Hills. We had been told that the world-famous landmark, the Hollywood sign, wasn't open to the public. It could be reached only by using a narrow dirt path on the side of the road. We were given detailed directions—but as it turned out, we didn't need them.

The path's entrance was mobbed with reporters.

"Vee's agent must have 'slipped' the location to the press," Frank muttered as we pushed our way through the crowd.

Ducking our heads down, we forged onward and ignored the reporters' questions.

"Do you think the killer will strike today?"

"What actions are you taking to protect Ms. Sharp?"

"Which one of you boys loves her the most?"

Moving up the dirt path, Frank and I approached the top of Mount Lee, the tallest peak in Los Angeles. The director, the cameraman, and the crew were already hard at work, setting up the final scene.

I looked up.

Cool.

There it was—the huge white blocky letters lined up in a long row overlooking the city: HOLLYWOOD.

I'd seen them on postcards and in movies. But they looked so much bigger close up.

Spider Jones, wearing a safari outfit and pith helmet, marched over to greet us. "Hello, guys," he said. "Did Vee come with you?"

"No," I told him.

He glanced down at his watch. "I *hope* she gets here *soon*. The wardrobe lady wants to do some *adjustments* on Vee's superhero costume."

He turned and walked away. Frank and I made our way along the length of the sign, staring up at the huge crane that swooped over the giant sign.

"So Vee is going to be hanging from that thing?" my brother asked.

"Yeah. She's supposed to be a girl superhero. Spider wants to shoot her flying past the Hollywood sign."

Frank sucked in his breath. "It sounds pretty risky."

"Yeah, I know."

I tried to tell myself that everything was going to be okay. The studio had hired extra security guards to keep an eye on things. And the crew assured us that Vee's harness had already been tested for safety purposes.

"Frank! Joe!"

We turned around and saw Jillian Goode standing at the end of the sign.

"Is Vee here yet?" she asked.

"No," we answered, walking toward her.

"Well, the killer is here," she told us.

I glanced at Frank. "What do you mean, Jillian?" he asked. "What makes you say that?"

She waved us forward. The three of us scrambled up the sloping hill behind the giant *H*. Then Jillian pointed to the back of the sign.

Someone had spray-painted the words: NUMBER 2: FALL FROM THE SKY.

But that wasn't all.

Underneath, it said: NUMBER 1: FALL OFF THE CHARTS.

"I guess that's all of them," said Frank. "The last of the Top Ten Ways to Die."

My stomach knotted up. I looked at my brother and said, "I guess this means that the killer is going to make his final move today."

Frank nodded. Jillian gripped him by the arm.

We turned our attention to the dirt path below us. The sound of motorcycle engines echoed in the valley. Spider Jones shouted something, so we scrambled down the hill to see what was going on.

Two motorcycles pulled up in front of the sign. The riders turned off their engines and pulled off their helmets.

It was Vee and her half sister Kay.

I slapped Frank's arm and laughed. "I didn't know Vee liked motorcycles."

Awesome.

We dashed over to greet them. Since Frank and I were motorcycle owners, we had a million questions to ask the Sharp sisters about their bikes.

"Check it out," said Vee. "I can receive e-mail messages on my dashboard!"

She pointed out the motorcycle's incredible features—which included a cell phone, Internet access, a personal date book, and a button to open the gates of her mansion.

"Man!" I said. "These are *killer* bikes!"

I could have kicked myself for using the word "killer," but Vee and Kay didn't seem to notice.

Before we could ask more questions, Spider Jones whisked Vee off to see the wardrobe lady. "Jump to it, my little *superstar*!" he gushed.

Kay grabbed the famous director and started telling him about her future plans to star in her own video. Frank and I used the opportunity to slip away and check up on the technical crew. We wanted to make sure Vee was going to be safe in her body harness.

The man in charge of the flying scene was a real pro. "Trust me," he told us. "This harness and crane could lift an elephant. There's nothing to worry about."

Still, I couldn't stop thinking about the warning on the back of the Hollywood sign.

FALL FROM THE SKY.

I stared up at the giant crane. Frank patted me on

the back. "Everybody's doing everything they can, Joe," he said. "Vee's going to be okay."

I was about to express my concerns when someone yelled my name.

"Joe! How do I look?"

I turned around. There was Vee—looking totally amazing in a tight pink and gold costume with a long flowing cape. Her hair was shorter and darker, which only made her look more beautiful. If that was possible.

"Vee! You look totally . . . super."

She laughed. "Thanks. The wardrobe lady really outdid herself, didn't she?" She spun around, waving her cape in the air.

"LISTEN UP, everyone!" Spider yelled. "Let's *do* this! *Vee!* Are you ready to get into the harness?"

"Ready as ever," she answered.

I couldn't take my eyes off her as she slipped into the body harness and prepared for the scene. The crew tugged on the wire, then gave a signal to the crane operator behind the sign.

"Ready? Lift her up!"

The crane whirred and Vee started rising up in the air. Higher and higher she went, until she floated forty feet over our heads.

"Look! I'm flying!" she shouted down to us. She twirled and swung back and forth gracefully.

"WONDERFUL, Vee!" Spider shouted up at her. "*CAMERAS!* Start rolling! I don't want to miss *any* of this!"

Vee tilted forward, with her hands pointing in front her. She swooped the air, then turned her head and smiled at the camera.

"EXCELLENT! EXCELLENT!" Spider yelled. "Do that *again*, Vee!"

I started to feel more comfortable as I watched her swing back and forth like a professional acrobat.

Wow, she's really good at this.

Then something strange happened.

The crane's engine roared and the giant metal arm jerked to the side.

Vee went flying.

The crane bobbed and jerked again. The sudden movement caused Vee to lose her balance. Her whole body flopped backward, sending her spinning and reeling through the air.

"What's going on?" I muttered.

The crane lurched. Vee screamed.

I watched helplessly as the metal arm of the crane jumped and swerved. Kicking and screaming, Vee went hurtling toward the sign so fast her body was almost a blur.

Suddenly it hit me.

She's going to crash!

16.
The Big Chase Scene

"Look out, Vee!" Joe shouted.

The pop star soared toward the sign, spinning out of control, and . . .

Wham!

Her feet crunched down against the giant *H* and cushioned the impact. Bending her knees, Vee shoved off the sign and went flying backward. The crane pivoted and lurched again.

"Whoooaaah!" Vee shrieked as she swooped through the air in a long arc. It looked like she was going to collide with the other end of the sign.

She's going to get killed, I thought.

"Come on, Joe!" I said, grabbing my brother's arm. "Let's see who's operating that crane!"

We charged up the hill and scrambled toward

SUSPECT PROFILE

Name: Theodore McMahon, aka "T-Mix"

Hometown: Chicago, IL

Physical description: 32 years old, 5'3", 125 lbs., dark hair worn in long braids, splotchy skin, flashy clothes.

Occupation: Record producer, sound mixer, songwriter

Background: Grew up in a bad neighborhood, shy and unpopular in school, studied music and electronics, went into the record business to become famous, developed an intense hatred for the singers he turned into stars.

Suspicious behavior: He was always around when Vee's life was threatened, was the last person in the studio when Brewster Fink was killed, was seen operating the crane behind the Hollywood sign.

Suspected of: Sending threatening notes to Vee Sharp, endangering her life, and murdering Brewster Fink.

Possible motives: Jealousy, envy, anger.

the back side of the sign. The crane was braced against the slope, chugging and grinding as it steered the long metal arm back and forth. As we ran toward it, I noticed someone lying on the ground a few feet away.

It was the crane operator. Somebody had knocked him unconscious!

"Who's moving the crane?" Joe asked, gasping.

We stepped over the operator and looked up at the seat of the crane. Sitting at the controls, laughing madly as he pulled the levers back and forth, was the last person we expected to see: T-Mix!

"Freeze!" I shouted.

The record producer snapped his head around and looked at us. His long braids hung down over his face—but they couldn't hide the evil glint in his eyes.

Joe and I reached up to grab him.

But T-Mix was too fast for us.

Hopping off the seat of the crane—and fortunately, braking it just before—he hit the ground and took off running down the hill.

Joe and I bolted after him, but it was hard to keep up. The guy was little but fast. As he disappeared around the end of the sign and pushed past the crew, I was afraid we were going to lose him.

"Frank! Over here!" Joe yelled. "The bikes!"

He pointed toward Vee and Kay's motorcycles. Without even hesitating, we jumped onto the bikes, revved them up, and zoomed down the dirt path after T-Mix.

He glanced back at us—and started running faster.

Joe and I rumbled over the bumps and dips of the steep terrain. Down the hill, faster and faster, we sped toward the highway below.

I didn't know what was going to happen when we reached the bottom. The road was crowded with trucks, cars, and reporters.

But that didn't stop T-Mix. He bent down like a running back at the Superbowl and hurtled head-first into the crowd.

"Hey! Look out!"

"Who is that guy?"

"He's crazy!"

The reporters scattered, opening a small path for T-Mix and our motorcycles. We steered the bikes right through the middle of the crowd without hurting anyone.

He's not getting away now, I thought.

T-Mix ran into the middle of the road, waving his arms at the approaching traffic. A large gray Cadillac screeched to a halt. T-Mix ran around the side of the car, flung open the door, and dragged the driver—Vee's agent, Jackson Puck—out of the seat.

T-Mix jumped behind the wheel and slammed the door. Then he gassed it, zooming off down the hill.

Jackson started shouting and shaking his fist at him. As Joe and I sped by on the motorcycles, I heard the agent yell, "If you get one scratch on my car, buddy, *I'm going to sue you!*"

The race was on.

T-Mix was about forty yards ahead of us, swerving back and forth on the long winding road. Joe and I crouched forward and increased our speed. We had to lean hard on the bikes—first right, then left, then right again—to make it through the swooping curves of the Hollywood Hills.

Suddenly my back tire skidded beneath me. For a second I thought I was going to go flying over the guardrail. But then I managed to steady my bike and turn my attention back to the chase.

T-Mix was only ten yards ahead of us now.

I glanced at the houses and lawns that lined the road. I immediately recognized where we were.

It's Vee's neighborhood.

As I passed by the huge mansions, I got an idea.

Signaling to Joe with my left hand, I pointed at

T-Mix's car and made a circular motion with my arm. I wasn't sure if my brother understood, but then he forged ahead in front of me and zoomed up next to the gray Cadillac.

That's it, Joe! Get ready.

We rounded a sharp curve. I spotted Vee's house in the distance. Then, glancing down at the dashboard, I pushed the button that opened Vee's front gate.

Yes! It's opening!

Joe knew exactly what to do. As soon as he and T-Mix reached the gated entrance, Joe swerved his bike—and forced T-Mix onto Vee's driveway.

We got him! He's trapped!

But T-Mix wasn't going to give up that easily.

Heading straight for Vee's front door, he suddenly slammed on the brakes and spun the car around. Then, hitting the gas, he took off across the lawn.

Clods of grass flew into the air. Joe and I swerved around them and screeched to a halt.

I glanced at my brother. "What do you think of this guy, Joe?"

"I think he should be put behind bars. And that's just for his driving."

We laughed and revved up our engines. Then we took off across the lawn after the Cadillac.

T-Mix drove like a maniac. Somehow he managed to mow down every plant, bush, and flower in Vee's Japanese garden.

Joe and I followed right behind him—but it wasn't easy. Every hill and stone was like a little ramp that sent our bikes soaring into the air and bouncing off the grass.

T-Mix steered the car around the side of the house and plowed his way toward the backyard. He was heading straight for a giant row of trimmed hedges.

He's going to crash, I thought.

But I was wrong. T-Mix turned the steering wheel at the last second. The car veered around the hedges and disappeared.

That's when I heard the splash.

A few seconds later, I heard T-Mix's voice.

"Help! Help!"

Joe and I guided our motorcycles around the hedge and pulled them to a quick stop.

"Help!"

T-Mix had driven the Jackson Puck's Cadillac right into Vee's swimming pool—and it was sinking fast.

"Help! I can't swim!"

I looked at Joe. "Well? Should we help him?"

Joe shrugged. "Sure, why not? I bet he'll write some really interesting songs in prison."

It didn't take long for the police to arrive—and the reporters, too. The whole place was swarming with people.

T-Mix kicked and squirmed as we held him down on the ground next to the pool. Joe and I were still soaking wet after saving him from the sinking car.

"Why did you do it?" Joe asked him. "Why did you want to hurt Vee? She's one of your biggest stars."

"Maybe she is," T-Mix sneered. "But I'm the biggest talent. She's just a pretty face. That's why she's famous. But I write the songs! I mix the tracks! I should be the famous one!"

A pair of police officers came running toward us, and a mob of photographers started snapping pictures.

"Well, here's your chance to be famous," said Joe.

"*Infamous* is more like it," I added.

T-Mix stared up at us with a wild look in his eyes. Then he started howling with laughter. Joe and I were relieved when the officers finally hand-cuffed him.

A crowd of people gathered around as the police escorted T-Mix to their squad car. Dozens of reporters started asking questions and taking pictures.

"Look at me!" T-Mix shouted at them. "I'm a star! I'm a *star*!"

The police pushed his head down and forced him into the back of the car. Then the door was slammed shut, and T-Mix was taken away.

Joe looked at me and shook his head. "That is one messed-up dude," he said.

"You think?"

"I *know*. But now I'm worried about Vee. We left her hanging over the Hollywood sign."

"Maybe this is her," I said, pointing toward the driveway.

A long black limousine drove past the reporters and stopped right in front of us. The door flew open, and out stepped Vee Sharp.

She was still wearing her superhero costume.

"Superwoman! You're okay!" Joe shouted.

Vee laughed, ran over, and gave us both a big hug.

"You guys are the real superheroes," she said. "How can I thank you?"

"Give them a kiss!" shouted a reporter.

Vee laughed again—and puckered her lips for the cameras. Flashbulbs flickered all around us as Vee kissed our cheeks.

Then I noticed other people climbing out of the limousine: Kay Sharp, Spider Jones, Jackson Puck, and Jillian Goode. They rushed over to greet us. Everyone was hugging and cheering— except for Jackson Puck, who wasn't too thrilled to hear about his Cadillac sitting at the bottom of Vee's pool.

After talking to the police and answering some questions from the press, Vee invited us all inside to celebrate the completion of the music video.

"We've all worked hard enough today," she announced. "It's party time!"

As we followed her into the mansion, my brother grabbed me by the arm and whispered in my ear, "Now *this* is what I call a Hollywood ending."

17.
Another Hollywood Ending

I miss her already.

That's what I started thinking as soon as we got back home to Bayport—and two weeks later, the feeling hadn't passed. Dad was sitting in his armchair doing a crossword puzzle, Mom was reading a book about ancient Egypt, Frank was finishing his homework, and Aunt Trudy was yelling at me to take my feet off the coffee table.

Where are you when I need you, Vee?

I held the TV remote in my hand and changed the channel to the VTV network.

"Here it is!" I said, sitting up. "Our music video is about to premiere!" They'd rushed it into production after T-Mix was caught.

I'd been waiting anxiously to see it. Dad put

down his crossword puzzle, Mom closed her book, and Frank pushed his homework aside. Even Aunt Trudy grabbed a spot on the sofa next to me.

"I'm curious to see what all the fuss is about," she said, adjusting her glasses.

Actually, the whole family was curious. Every news program in the country had shown pictures of Frank and me getting kissed by Vee in her super-hero outfit. Every day the press had more juicy details about the "Pop Star Stalker" and his "Top Ten Ways to Die."

Frank and I were a little nervous about all the publicity. A few reporters had even called here at the house to interview us. Thankfully, Aunt Trudy told them they had the wrong Hardys.

"It still scares me to think about that weirdo," said Mom. "What are the chances that you boys would be working side by side with a killer?"

The chances are good—when you're undercover agents, I thought to myself.

Of course I didn't tell her that. I just cranked up the volume on the TV so we could hear the veejay introduce Vee's new video.

A guy with spiky blond hair appeared on the screen. "Tonight's a very special night for fans of America's biggest teen pop sensation, Vee Sharp. I'm sure you've heard about what happened to the young star two weeks ago. After receiving a number of anonymous death threats, Vee was nearly killed in a series of mysterious 'accidents' on the set of her new music video. Vee managed to survive, and the culprit was apprehended—thanks to a pair of brave teenage interns."

A picture of Frank and me flashed across the screen. I nudged Frank. "You should have smiled, dude."

"Look who's talking," he said. "You have red-eye."

Aunt Trudy shushed us. "The video's about to start," she said.

I looked at her. "Since when are *you* a Vee Sharp fan, Aunt Trudy?"

She smiled primly. "Actually, I like her new song. I heard it on the radio today."

"Well, maybe I can introduce you to her. I have connections, you know."

She slapped my arm. "Shhh."

We turned our attention back to the blond-haired announcer on TV. "The legendary record producer, T-Mix, has confessed to the crimes and is being held without bail. For Vee Sharp, the nightmare is over. And what better way to celebrate than to introduce the brand-new video of her number one hit single, 'Girls Rule.'"

The picture changed to a video message from

Vee Sharp. She looked straight at the camera and said, "Hi, everyone. It's me, Vee. I just want to thank you all for the love and support I've received during these tough times. But most of all, I want to thank Joe and Frank. This one's for you."

The screen went black. The video started.

A heavy beat pounded and throbbed from the TV speakers. Beautiful images flashed before our eyes. It was like reliving our whole experience in Hollywood. I couldn't help but smile. There she was—Vee—as a black widow spider, a mermaid, an astronaut, a lion tamer, and a superhero.

Hey, if anyone could prove that "Girls Rule," she could.

Suddenly I heard the flapping of wings overheard. Playback, our parrot, swooped into the living room and landed right on top of the TV set.

"Check it out!" said Frank. "I knew that bird was a big Vee Sharp fan!"

Playback squawked, "Joe loves Vee Sha-arp! Joe loves Vee Sha-arp!"

I groaned and covered my eyes. "Why did you teach him that, Frank?"

"Because it's true."

I ignored him and watched the rest of the video. Vee looked totally cool swimming in the giant goldfish bowl and cracking the whip at the lions. I practically forgot that she had almost been killed in every scene.

All of a sudden, my face appeared on the screen.

"Look! It's Joe!" Aunt Trudy squealed with delight.

Everybody laughed and cheered. Frank punched me playfully in the arm as I slumped down deeper into the sofa. Seeing myself in those powder blue pajamas was a little embarrassing.

"Awww. You look *so* cute, Joe," said Mom. "Just like a little boy."

Okay, it was *very* embarrassing.

But what the heck, I figured. I was in a Vee Sharp video!

Finally the video ended. The whole family clapped their hands. Mom gave Frank a hug, and Aunt Trudy kissed my cheek. Then Dad looked at us and said, "Good job, boys."

I could tell by the look in his eye that he was congratulating us on our latest assignment.

He was the only one who knew how much danger we'd been in.

Suddenly there was a knock at the door.

"I hope that isn't a bunch of reporters," said Dad.

"Oh, it's probably a group of screaming girls," said Aunt Trudy. "I'm sure your fans are dying for your autographs. Why don't you answer the door, Joe?"

There was a strange twinkle in her eye, but I ignored it and walked to the front door. Reaching for the knob, I opened the door slowly and peeked out.

No way.

I couldn't believe my eyes.

It was Vee Sharp! Here! In Bayport!

"Hello, Joe," she said, smiling that world-famous smile.

"Vee! What . . . where . . . how?" I stammered.

Vee shrugged her shoulders. "I just happened to be in the neighborhood."

"You're kidding."

"Of course I'm kidding. Bayport isn't exactly the crossroads of the world. And that's *exactly* why I'm here."

"What do you mean?"

Vee sighed and pushed a strand of hair off her face. "If you invite me inside, Joe, maybe I'll tell you."

"Oops. Sorry. Come in!"

I was so shocked to see her that I could barely think straight. Stepping back to let her inside, I ushered her into the living room to introduce her to my family.

"Mom, Dad, Aunt Trudy, I'd like you to meet . . ."

"Vee Sharp," said Aunt Trudy. "It's a pleasure to finally meet you. I'm a big fan. Come sit next to me!"

I glanced at Frank and stifled a laugh.

Vee took a seat on the sofa and explained why she was here. "The press is having a field day with the whole 'Pop Star Stalker' story. There are reporters and cameras everywhere I go. They just won't leave me alone. It's crazy. After that whole experience, I just want to get away from it all."

I still didn't understand how she'd found her way here to Bayport.

"Everybody wanted to interview me for the video premiere tonight," Vee continued. "My hairstylist, Betty, told me I should take a break and spend some time where no one could find me. She said she had a good friend on the East Coast who might let me visit for a few days."

She looked at Aunt Trudy and smiled.

Suddenly it hit me.

Betty?

"Wait a minute," I said, turning to Aunt Trudy. "Your friend Betty in L.A. is Vee's hairstylist?"

Aunt Trudy leaned back and smirked. "I have connections, you know," she said.

I couldn't believe it. Aunt Trudy had invited Vee to stay with us until the whole 'Pop Star Stalker' thing cooled down.

"Did Mom and Dad know about this?" I asked.

They all nodded.

I shook my head and laughed. "This is great! So how long are you staying?"

"Four or five days."

"Where are your bags?"

"On the front porch."

"How cool is this?"

"Very cool."

Vee smiled again. I was so excited I just wanted to hug her.

But first Frank and I had to go outside to get her luggage. As soon as we were alone, I grabbed him by the arm and said, "This is too good to be true, Frank. I was afraid I'd never see her again, but this is my chance to really get to know her. So please, don't ruin it for me."

My brother looked surprised. "What are you talking about?"

"You know. Don't pull any pranks while she's here. Don't make me look stupid. Don't make fun of me in front of her."

"Whatever you say . . ."

"Frank."

"Don't worry, man. I won't say anything to embarrass you. I promise."

We picked up Vee's luggage and went back inside the house. Aunt Trudy had moved Vee into the dining room, where she was ladling out a big help-

168